WISH
UPON A
DUKE

JR SALISBURY

OLIVER HEBER BOOKS

Cover Design by Wicked Smart Designs

Published by Oliver-Heber Books

0 9 8 7 6 5 4 3 2 1

CHAPTER 1

Rain, the relentless, nonstop rain, continued to pelt down on the carriage as it had for the past two days. "Typical spring weather" was what she'd been told by the coachman after the first day. Fortunately, she had been able to afford to rent a carriage to take them to their new home, Sky View, on the southwest coast of England.

She glanced to the seat across from her, where her seven-year-old son, Vincent, lay sleeping. The boy had done remarkably well through all this. First his father died unexpectedly, then she received word that his uncle had also died in a mysterious hunting accident. As he'd never married or had children of his own, this left her son the current Earl of Dorset.

Her mother-in-law had pleaded with her to bring Vincent to England so he could be groomed for his role. She had done this twice. The first time when Roland had died, the second, of course, when Timothy, the earl at the time, was shot and killed in a hunting accident. The earldom could have been passed to some obscure cousin living in the north of England, but it was time. Time for Vincent to take his rightful place.

It had been an easy decision to make. Though her

own parents adored Vincent, they understood their young grandson's station in life. Not to mention her father saw the wealth the earldom would provide for his daughter and grandson. Being a lawyer and politician respectively, Roland and James Kennedy had shared many a bottle of fine brandy discussing how the British aristocracy would have to expand their business interests from simple tenant farming to interests outside their estates.

That need had been in part what brought Roland to America. He saw the potential, the new opportunities to secure his future. Investing in shipping, the building of ships, as well as bringing spices and sugar from the Caribbean, Roland had made a fortune for himself and his family. Until he was lost at sea and left Savannah a widow. A very wealthy young widow. Her father had overseen the sale of the foundry and businesses on her behalf. Then came the news from England, and she made the hardest decision of her life. To take Vincent back to England to claim his birthright.

Her father had forewarned her of people wanting to take over her son's upbringing, as his life would now drastically change. Though she was tougher than she appeared, Savannah was well aware of the hierarchy and how women fit in. He had told her to stand her ground if something didn't seem right.

She stared out the window at the lush rolling countryside as the rain continued to pelt down and she prayed for the strength to see this through. She was the outsider. Now she would know how Roland must have felt when he first arrived in America. Then again, he had been an educated man with money. Men were always viewed differently.

To make matters worse, she had no one on her side. Though her mother-in-law would want what was best for Vincent, Savannah was sure she would have ulterior motives. Roland had told her enough about his mother throughout the years. She was known for her sharp tongue and ruthless ways, and how one must keep their guard up when around the countess.

Her father had given her the name of a man he and Roland did business within London. He told her on the day of their departure that he had written the gentleman, and should she have any questions or problems to contact said gentleman in London. She had tucked his name into a journal she kept, which now contained crucial information her father had discovered about the estate through the family solicitors. How much they were actually sharing was beyond her, but since her father was acting as the boy's American representative, she had little doubt they'd withhold much.

She wished her father had been able to come with them, just to see them settled in and to check everything out. Her mother had been in ill health herself for the past several months, which solidified her father's wish to remain in America. Savannah would make it on her own, take meticulous notes, and ask all the right questions. She was still the boy's mother, and she would make sure he didn't have his future taken away from him,

Vincent would be schooled at home until he was old enough to be sent to a boys' school, where he would learn things not even she could teach him. Education had been another topic Roland had discussed with her. Even though Roland wasn't the heir, his father made sure his second son was well schooled in case he ever needed to take over the role as earl. That had proven to be wise, as Roland's brother, Timothy, had suffered an early demise.

It would be hard at first for her son. He would not have many playmates or friends. At least not until he went off to school. She knew that would be a difficult adjustment for him to have to make.

She wondered what would become of her once Vincent was on a schedule. Until he went to boarding school, Savannah intended to stay as close to her son as possible. She wondered if the dowager countess still resided at the family home or if she resided elsewhere. The dowager countess made no mention of anything except Vincent and his future in her many letters.

Suddenly, the carriage slowed and made a left turn. Though she couldn't see the manor home, Savannah was aware they were now on the family estate. The long drive leading to the house was covered with stone. Trees lined either side, and beyond that stretched a combination of wooded areas and green fields. Even through the rain, she could tell the property was well maintained. The estate boasted fields of meadowsweet, sun-dried grass nearer the ocean, and thick forests throughout the back of the acreage. As the carriage pulled to a stop at the manor house, Savannah could only stare in awe. She'd seen fine large houses in America, but nothing as grand as this. Sky View was indeed far more incredible than the homes of the new rich in New York, Boston, or Rhode Island.

She reached across the carriage and shook Vincent ever so slightly on the shoulder. The boy's sable-brown hair was tousled from tossing and turning. Slowly, his coffee-colored eyes opened. He sat up, rubbed his eyes, and looked out the window.

"Are we here, Mama?" he asked, wide-eyed.

She nodded. "Yes, we are finally home, my lord."

He giggled at the way she addressed him. Though she'd covered many topics with her young son, it would take far more to turn this American-born-and-bred boy into an earl. It would be worth it.

The large oak front door opened as she and Vincent exited the carriage, and a tall, well-dressed older man appeared. The butler, Savannah mused. She held on to Vincent's hand as he stood in awe of that grand home.

"I am Savannah Dawson, and this is my son, Vincent, the new Earl of Dorset," she said in a clear, steady voice.

The butler stood at the top of the stairs waiting. "I am Higgins. We've been expecting you, madam. Welcome to Sky View."

This was the moment she'd been dreading. There was no turning back. Still holding Vincent's hand, she began walking up the stairs, her back straight as befitted the regal woman she knew she was. She and Roland might not have lived in the manner in which he was raised, but Vincent was now an earl, and she would be damned if anyone would damage her late husband's memory.

At the top of the stairs, she followed the butler inside. Trying not to stare, Savannah felt in awe of the elegant surroundings. She'd never seen an entrance hall quite like it. The ceiling stood far above them, with an imposing grand staircase descending from the floor above. A magnificent fresco graced the ceiling.

Higgins paused. "If you will follow me, I'll show you to the blue drawing room and let the dowager countess know you've arrived."

"Thank you, Higgins," she replied as she followed the aging butler up the stairs.

Still holding Vincent's hand, she continued to follow him to two massive oak doors. A footman stood in red-and-gold livery to one side of the door. Seeing the butler, the young man opened the door. Vincent stared with wide eyes. It was almost too much for either of them to take in. The room was decorated in various shades of blue, with gold for an accent color.

While warm and inviting, Savannah found it almost pretentious.

The butler had disappeared in search of Roland's mother, Vincent's grandmother, Eloisa, the Dowager Countess of Dorset. While Roland had depicted his mother as strict and for the most part unloving, Savannah prayed the woman would accept Vincent and her. The dowager countess had not been too enthused upon learning she had an American daughter-in-law. To her, Savannah was nothing more than a common tavern wench, not to mention she wasn't happy her son had married an American, which she let Roland know in every letter.

Sitting down on a gold brocade couch, Savannah encouraged her young son to do the same. He sat next to her, his eyes still wide as saucers.

"Mama, is this where we're going to live?"

"Yes, darling. We've discussed this. This is your father's family home, and it is now ours, remember?"

"Yes. I'm the earl," he said proudly. He smiled and surveyed his new surroundings.

The sound of the door being opened and the swish of skirts caused Savannah to glance back across the room. A petite woman in her early fifties walked toward them. Her brown eyes stood out against her salt-and-pepper hair.

Savannah swallowed hard. She would never meet the woman's expectations. It was evident in her expression she showed Savannah as she peered from her to Vincent, then back.

"Horrible day for travel, but I see you both made it safely," the dowager countess observed.

"Yes, we're happy to be here, Lady Dorset," Savannah replied. "It was a difficult journey."

Ignoring her, the older woman focused her attention on Vincent. "You look so much like your father. You may call me Grandmother."

Vincent nodded, saying nothing.

"The boy can't speak?"

"Of course he can speak," Savannah replied. "He's simply overwhelmed by all the changes."

"I'll ring for his governess to come take him to the nursery," the dowager countess said, apparently without a second thought as to what Savannah had just told her.

"You've already hired a governess?"

"Of course I have. I've hired a tutor as well, but we can discuss all that over tea."

Higgins entered the room and stood, waiting on the older woman's instructions.

"Have Miss West show my grandson to the nursery. I'm sure he's hungry."

"Yes, my lady. Anything else?"

"Mrs. Dawson and I will have tea before she's shown to her rooms."

"Very well," Higgins replied, and disappeared as quietly as he had appeared.

Savannah remained quiet, not knowing what to say to her mother-in-law. She had the distinct feeling the older woman was not going to be easily won over.

After a few minutes of awkward silence, a young blonde woman appeared.

"Miss West," the Dowager Lady Dorset said, "this is my grandson, Vincent. Why don't you show him to the nursery? His mother and I have much to discuss."

Miss West offered her hand to Vincent. "Come, Master Vincent. I'll show you to your new room."

Vincent cautiously eyed his governess, then glanced at his mother for approval. Savannah hoped he didn't cause a scene, though on second thought, it might be just the thing to introduce his grandmother to how American-raised boys acted.

"Go on. Go with Miss West," Savannah encouraged. "I'll see you shortly."

"But I want to stay with you, Mama."

"I know you do, but remember what we talked about? You're now the Earl of Dorset, and with that comes new responsibilities and changes. I'm sure you and Miss West will become fast friends."

"Very well," he replied sullenly. He walked over to take Miss West's outstretched hand. Savannah's heart beat a little quicker seeing her son leave with someone she just met. The door opened once again, this time the butler entered with a footman, carrying a tray with cups, saucers, and a pot of tea.

"Come," the dowager countess said as the door closed. "How do you take your tea?"

Savannah didn't say anything for a moment, and then felt the older woman staring at her. "I'm sorry. It's just that Vincent and I have been together since his father died, and it's hard to watch him walk off with someone else."

"Then you have many adjustments to make."

"Yes, you're right."

She accepted a cup of tea Lady Dorset had made her without waiting for her response to her earlier question.

The older woman stirred sugar into her tea. "Vincent will be fine. He has much to learn, as I'm sure you are aware."

"Yes, Roland had shared with me his upbringing…"

"His education was different from that of his brother, as shall be Vincent's. He's the earl now, and that means changes."

"He still needs to be a little boy," Savannah said softly.

"He has responsibilities."

"What sort of responsibility can a seven-year-old boy have? He needs to be schooled to learn what's expected of him when he takes on his role of earl."

"Ah, you have much to learn about the English aristocracy." The dowager countess picked up her cup of tea and took a polite sip.

"I understand the family solicitors are overseeing everything until Vincent is old enough?"

Lady Dorset nodded. "The estate manager here will run the estate, as will the estate managers of the other two holdings."

"I would like to be allowed to oversee the ledgers on behalf of Vincent, of course."

She arched a gray brow. "That is highly unusual."

"But not unheard of?"

"No, I suppose not. I can assure you the earldom will be well looked after until Vincent comes of age."

Savannah said nothing and took a sip of tea.

"I have enlisted the help of the Duke of Clevedon to assist with Vincent's education. He lives in the estate next to Sky View."

"Why would you do that?" Savannah asked.

"Because the boy needs a father figure, someone besides tutors to teach him how to hunt and fish and ride a horse. In fact, I've invited the duke to dinner tonight. I thought the sooner he meets you and young Vincent, the better."

"You want a stranger to teach my son?"

"Clevedon is hardly a stranger, my dear. He was Roland's best friend for many, many years. I simply asked him to help with the boy's upbringing, and he enthusiastically agreed."

Too many decisions were being made for her in the raising of her son. Unfortunately, some of the points her mother-in-law brought up were valid. Vincent did need a strong male figure to look up to, and if Lady Dorset thought the duke was suitable, then she should too, though she'd reserve any decision until she met the duke.

"Then I look forward to meeting the duke and hearing his thoughts on how my son should be raised."

"Excellent." Lady Dorset beamed, but then she appraised Savannah's dress with disdain. "You'll need a more suitable wardrobe. I'm afraid your current one won't suffice in your new role."

"How's that?"

"Americans are behind in fashion. What you wear is out-of-date. No worry. My modiste will come from London to fit you. I'll send for her immediately."

Savannah was going to protest, but she had the feeling that would do her no good, at least not now. She needed to give everything some time before she began to make her own changes.

"Very well. If you don't mind, I'd like to go to my rooms. I'd like to rest before dinner."

"Of course. Let me get Mrs. Hatcher to show you the way. Did you bring a lady's maid?"

Savannah smiled. "No, I'm afraid I didn't. The one I had didn't want to leave her family by moving all the way to England."

"I'll have Mrs. Hatcher find someone temporarily. Then you can find someone permanently."

Having her own maid, except on occasions where she needed help dressing, was not something she truly desired. She didn't cherish the idea of having to wear a corset more often than she was accustomed to.

Lady Dorset rose and walked to the bellpull before sitting back in her chair. "I look forward to getting to know you and my grandson better," she said without a smile.

Savannah wasn't so sure about that. The older

woman seemed more interested in seeing to Vincent's immediate needs than Savannah's. The disdain in her voice just now made it evident Lady Dorset was going to make life difficult. "Will Vincent be allowed to join us at dinner this evening?"

The countess stared at her in shock, as though she'd said something blasphemous. "Heavens, no. He'll take his meals in the nursery."

"But won't the duke want to meet his new charge?"

"The duke will meet him another time."

She was going to ask more about this duke, but Mrs. Hastings reappeared.

"Mrs. Hastings, would you show Mrs. Dawson to her rooms? I believe she'd like to rest awhile before dressing for dinner."

"Yes, madam." She eyed Savannah curiously. "If you'll follow me, I'll take you to your rooms."

Lady Dorset said, "She'll also need a lady's maid, if you can find a girl temporarily until someone suitable can be hired."

"Miss Abbott will suit perfectly," the housekeeper replied.

"The upstairs maid? Yes, she would be more than capable."

"I have her unpacking for you now," she said, glancing at Savannah. "I think you'll like her."

CHAPTER 2

Gabriel Armstrong, twelfth Duke of Clevedon, sat back in his chair, estate ledgers lying open on the desk in front of him. Though he had an extremely competent estate manager who kept the ledgers up-to-date, Gabriel himself liked to review everything before his once-a-month meeting with Harold Bottoms, a man whose father had been estate manager at Brook Fall for his entire adult life. The two men met weekly, more if there was something requiring Gabriel's immediate attention. Other than that, Bottoms kept himself busy on the estate. Brook Fall wasn't small by any means. It graced the English countryside with magnificent meadows and forests, encompassing nearly twenty thousand acres.

The estate had been the ducal family seat for over four hundred years, making it one of the oldest in all England, and it was where Gabriel preferred to spend his time. London held no appeal for him. He tried to make sure his trips to Town were quick, staying only long enough to take care of whatever business might need completing. But then there was the Season. Every mother wanted nothing more than to see her daughter married to him, which was precisely why he never let on he was indeed in the market for a wife. He tolerated various balls, soirees, and dinner parties, but as far as anyone knew, he was there only at the invitation of the host.

Finding a wife, a woman who would be his duchess, had proven more complicated than he first anticipated. He for feared every debutante would be lined up waiting to catch his attention, Instead, he quietly paid attention to who attended each event.

He wanted a woman who was both intelligent and pleasing to the eyes. She didn't have to be beautiful, as he often found the beauties were either lacking in intelligence or they put themselves above everyone else around them. Most who fell into that category were clingy, trying their best to win his favor and attention.

The woman who became his duchess would have to be kind and considerate, and someone with whom he could converse. He disliked having to speak about the weather or the latest gossip. He detested gossip and wanted nothing to do with women who enjoyed it. She would also have to be willing to pick up the reins of the charities his late mother had started which provided clothing, food, and education for the children living on the estate with their families or in the village.

A knock on the door caused him to slip back into reality.

"Come," he said.

The door opened, and his long-time butler, Simmons, appeared. The man, like his estate manager, was not the first in his family to hold his position. Simmons's father and grandfather had both served as butlers at Brook Fall.

"I'm sorry to disturb you, Your Grace, but this just arrived from Lady Dorset," he said, presenting a small silver tray to Gabriel.

Gabriel nodded and scanned the contents of the note. "Is someone waiting for a reply?"

"Yes, Your Grace. I sent him to the kitchens to wait."

"Very well, give me five minutes to write a reply, and tell Cook there is no need to make dinner. It appears I'll be dining with the dowager countess. Her grandson, the new earl, and her daughter-in-law have finally arrived."

"I'll tell Cook not to prepare dinner and return for your reply, Your Grace. Anything else?"

"No, that'll be all, Simmons."

He pulled out a fresh sheet of paper as the butler silently left the room. Moving one of the ledgers out of his way, he began to compose his reply. Though he wasn't in the mood to dine with the countess and listen to her rave on about members of the peerage, he knew he needed to. He'd agreed to assist in the schooling of the young earl.

How old was the boy? Quite young, perhaps six or seven. Though Gabriel hadn't had many dealings with children, he found himself eager to embark upon his new adventure. He'd been taken aback at first when the countess had come to him, but understood her reasoning after learning there weren't any other male relatives remotely near the estate who could serve as a mentor to Roland's son. He couldn't wait to spend time with the boy.

Simmons reappeared and took the silver tray, which now included the duke's reply. Gabriel rose from his chair and walked to the windows. It was still raining, though far less than it had for the past few days. Being cooped up in the house like this unsettled him. He preferred riding his horse and checking on the estate. There was always something going on, and Gabriel couldn't envision any other place to spend his time than at Brook Fall.

At a table near his desk which held crystal decanters, he poured himself a brandy and returned to his seat. The countess was holding dinner at seven, which meant it would be an early evening. That was another thing he didn't miss about London. Dinners started late, for the most part, and took hours to complete. He was usually seated next to or near a young single woman, something he abhorred. The only thing good about his position at functions like this was that he was among the first, if not *the* first, to be seated. Given his family's history, he was usually the senior ranking member in attendance.

He swirled the glass before taking a long swallow of the French brandy he'd had shipped home after his last visit to Paris. No one could quite make brandy, wine, or champagne like the French, and he had a cellar full to prove it.

His mind wandered back to the young boy, Vincent. Would he favor his old friend Roland, or would he resemble his American-born mother? Gabriel had heard countless stories about her, not only from the countess, but from the late earl, Roland's brother, Timothy. Both had been beside themselves when Roland accepted a position as a partner in an American foundry. The countess thought Roland was being disloyal to his family. As a second son, it was not only his right, but his destiny to choose what he would do in life. He accepted no money from his brother, not that he'd had an allowance to begin with when he left for America. That was the one thing Timothy had done out of spite: cut off Roland's allowance. Through savvy business dealings, Roland had nevertheless built a fortune of his own.

Gabriel had known Timothy almost as well as he'd known Roland. Being that they were brothers, one would have thought they would have been closer in personality. Instead, Gabriel found Timothy reckless and uncaring. Certainly, he himself had been raised to believe that as duke, he would be above everyone else. Timothy had been raised similarly, but he had a cruel, vindictive streak, and his brother paid dearly. Roland became the victim of his brother's wicked side and found himself at school unable to avoid the wrath of his brother or his friends. At home, it had been easier for Roland because he could ride his horse across the estate and not be found. Gabriel and Roland had become fast friends through their mutual love of horses.

Gabriel shuddered at the thought of Timothy's cruelty. No one had been safe from him, not his siblings nor the boys at school nor servants. Anyone who dared cross him at the wrong time had paid the price, and dearly. Timothy might not get his vengeance that moment, but he would instead wait until his unsuspecting prey was caught off guard, much like an animal on the hunt. Gabriel had never been on that receiving end of Timothy's machinations as there seemed to be an unspoken vow between the two. It almost seemed that Timothy knew that Gabriel's rank made him untouchable.

Timothy's death had been due to a mysterious hunting accident, which shocked a few. He was known to be an avid hunter, and his hunting parties were famous. The estate always had plenty of game for Timothy's guests, and he was usually the one to lead the parties out each morning. Gabriel had been invited to several until he'd mentioned—perhaps, in Timothy's eyes, complained—about his host's reckless manner with his rifle. After that, the invitations quit coming.

Gabriel had only been to Sky View twice since Timothy's death. Once to pay his condolences upon the news of the earl's death, and the second to visit with the countess when she approached him with the idea of him mentoring Roland's young son, now the Earl of Dorset.

Tonight would be his third. A small dinner affair to welcome Roland's widow and son home, and to give Gabriel an opportunity to meet his small charge. The idea was still odd to him. He'd never given much thought to children. Yes, he wanted children of his own at some point, but to be asked to help with the raising of someone else's child gave him pause.

Then there was the young earl's mother. He knew little about her. Most of what he'd learned had come from his correspondence with Roland. She was American, her father a wealthy industrialist. Roland had loved her deeply, which was a far cry from what the countess felt. It had never sat well with her that her second son would marry an American, let alone a commoner. The dowager countess thought America was full of savages and that they were lacking in social skills. She had mentioned more than once that she couldn't wait for her grandson to arrive so she could make his Americanisms disappear, which would be impossible, because Vincent's mother could never change who she was.

He would have to monitor closely to make sure the countess didn't attempt to undermine her daughter-in-law. He intended to get to know Mrs. Dawson better, as it would be to their advantage to play on the same team, so to speak. The dowager countess would have to be monitored and kept from fulfilling her own agenda, which would be to send her daughter-in-law back to America.

It must have taken a great deal of courage for Mrs. Dawson to leave her own family and set out on a new life to see her son raised as an earl should be. Roland had obviously educated his wife quite well in how the aristocracy worked, never imagining that it would be put to good use when his own young son quite unexpectedly became earl. He imagined she must be a strong woman to accept such responsibility. He'd always been in awe of women who were able to rise to any occasion. Savannah Dawson certainly sounded like this sort of woman.

His thoughts were abruptly interrupted by a quick knock on the door, followed by the Earl of Wexford pushing past a flustered Simmons. Gabriel and Wexford had been fast friends at Eton and Cambridge, part of a small group of heirs sent to the finest schools to prepare them for their future responsibilities.

"Wexford!" Gabriel exclaimed. He shut the two remaining ledgers that lay open. One thing about Wexford, he was a bit too curious about the goings-on of those around him.

"I tried to tell Simmons here you wouldn't mind being interrupted."

"What brings you to Brook Fall on a such a miserable day?"

The earl arranged his lanky frame in one of the overstuffed leather chairs in front of Gabriel's desk. With his blond hair and piercing blue eyes, he always reminded Gabriel of a Norseman. Or was it a Viking? "I was nearby, heading back to London after visiting my sister Helen and her family."

Gabriel rose from behind his desk and walked to the sideboard where his liquor decanters sat. "Brandy?"

Wexford nodded, saying nothing.

"How is your sister?" Gabriel asked. "I don't believe I've seen her recently."

"That's because she's with child again and spends most of her time confined to the house."

Gabriel poured a healthy splash of brandy into each of the snifters and passed one to Wexford. "What is this, her fourth child?"

Wexford accepted the glass, nodding. "Yes, and each one is more difficult than the previous. Four children in five years? Poor Helen hasn't had a year's rest," Wexford replied. "I understand Burton wanting an heir, but he's become fanatical about the whole thing."

"Perhaps they'll get lucky this time and have a son, then Burton will not visit her bed so often."

"One can hope," he said, then tossed back the brandy. Wexford and his sister, along with their brother, Tom, had had a trying childhood. Their father had preferred his drink over his family. Children were meant to be seen and not heard and, most importantly, be raised by others. Thus his friend had been sent to Eton at a very young age. His family never visited, and it was rare for him to go home during any holiday breaks. It had been easy for him, Roland, and Wexford to become fast friends.

"Has your protégé arrived?"

"Yes, he and his mother arrived today, and he's not my protégé, Parr." Parr was what Gabriel and everyone else called Wexford in private, rather than his given or secondary names. They were stuffy old monikers that he refused to use.

"When do you plan on meeting them?"

"The countess is having me for dinner this evening for exactly that purpose."

Parr snorted. "Of course, you're eager for this meeting?"

Gabriel swallowed some brandy and gazed thoughtfully at his friend. "Yes, I am."

"And his mother?"

"His mother as well, since she will be the one I deal with in regard to the boy. The dowager countess, as you know, is the one who requested my help with him."

"At least the boy's young enough to still rid him of any bad habits."

Gabriel nodded. "Knowing Roland, the boy has had the start of a decent education. Nothing like he'll receive here, of course, but he won't be running wild and disobedient."

"I don't envy you."

"Neither do I, but it'll be worth it in the long term," Gabriel said as he glanced at a clock. It was time to make himself ready for dinner. "You're welcome to stay the night. I'm sure Cook can come up with a decent enough dinner for you."

"That's much appreciated. Thank you."

"No need. The weather hasn't been the best for traveling. Feel free to make yourself at home. Since the boy and his mother arrived just today, I doubt it'll be a long night. Perhaps you'll indulge me in a game of chess later?"

Parr grinned and swirled the remaining brandy in his glass. "I can't wait to beat you yet again."

"Says a man who hated the game a year ago."

Parr laughed loudly and finished his brandy. "Let me allow you to dress for your dinner. I'll have your man show my valet to my room, if he hasn't done so already."

"I'll see you later for that game of chess," Gabriel replied. He stood from behind the desk, and locked the ledgers in a desk drawer before he walked toward the door, Parr following. He left Parr speaking with Simmons, then quickly made his way up the stairs, down the hall to his room. Inside, he found Burns laying out his clothes for the evening. The man knew what Gabriel wanted—sometimes even before he did. It was almost eerie how well he understood Gabriel's needs.

Good valets took years to learn their master's preferences, but Burns was exceptional. He never overstepped his bounds and had served Gabriel well, even becoming a very trusted servant and confidant. The man had certainly seen him in not the best of conditions quite a few times, especially after Gabriel's father, the former duke, died.

"Your Grace, I have everything ready for your bath."

"Thank you, Burns. I have enough time for a long soak in the tub," he replied. "Also, beware, Parr is spending the night. Hopefully, he won't pull any pranks."

Parr had always been the jokester among their friends, and Gabriel had learned early on not to trust him in situations such as this. He might find himself soaked in water upon entering his own rooms when he returned this evening, the victim of a pail of water strategically placed above the doorframe. Nothing was sacred when Parr the prankster was around.

His mind was filled with questions, more about Roland's widow than the boy. What sort of woman was she? She was American after all. He'd heard American women were bold and daring compared to most of their English counterparts. Was she pleasing to look at? Remembering his friend Roland's taste in women, his wife would be a beauty.

CHAPTER 3

Savannah barely listened as Miss Abbott, the lady's maid the countess assigned her, prattled on and on. Occasionally, she would pick up a snippet of how quiet the house had been since the late young earl had died, or how well-liked Lady Dorset was, how charitable she was, or even how she knew the house inside and out.

Drivel was the word that went through Savannah's mind. The girl had probably never had much experience dressing a lady, and Savannah was slightly uncomfortable having someone to assist her. But this was how the English did things, so she'd better adapt. Life was no longer as it once was, and for Vincent's sake, she had to put her own feelings aside.

She walked over to the mirror to make sure everything was in place and that she appeared presentable. Tonight, the Duke of Clevedon was coming to dinner. Why on her first night here, Savannah couldn't fathom, but the dowager countess had set everything up, and Savannah would play her part. She was quite curious about the duke and wanted to know more about him. He would be spending considerable time with Vincent, and that was enough. He would make him a proper

English lord, which made Savannah fear she would lose the sweet young boy she loved.

"You look quite lovely, my lady. The color becomes you," Abbott said, beaming.

"Thank you. I do love the color."

The gown was a deep rose, the bodice lower than what she usually preferred. She'd tried not to feign shock the first time she caught a glimpse of herself. She hadn't realized how out of fashion most all her wardrobe was. She would have to venture to London to remedy that situation.

There were also other matters needing her attention in London. She needed to make an appointment to meet with Roland's solicitors. She'd already been in touch with them when she realized she would be moving to England. Though she had a good idea of what Roland had left them, she decided to stay involved. She had read every report that had come out about Roland's businesses in England, along with his American interests. Though most women would shy away from figures and reports, Savannah welcomed them. She'd made a promise to herself when Roland died not to take any man's word about how Roland's investments were doing.

Many men thought woman were simply another piece of property and treated them as such. Roland had been far more forward-thinking. He knew his wife to be capable far beyond just keeping the household books. He'd known she could easily handle anything that came her way. Already, she had a list of questions to ask the solicitor when she met with him. More would follow, she was sure, as she became acquainted with her new life changes.

"You best go downstairs, my lady. The dowager countess doesn't like anyone being late."

Savannah nodded and placed her hand over the

double strand of pearls Roland had given her for their last anniversary. Turning from the mirror, she walked across the room to the door.

A few minutes later, she stood in front of the drawing room, where a red-liveried footman opened the door. Everything was so formal here.

The dowager countess sat near the fire, a tall man with golden-brown hair talking with her. Savannah was taken with the way the red highlights in his hair shone in the firelight. He appeared to be muscular, which she thought was odd. She knew from what her husband had told her that most Englishmen preferred to spend their time indoors. The duke appeared to enjoy the outdoors. His eyes met hers for a moment before the dowager countess interrupted.

Savannah was tardy, and the censure in Lady Dorset's eyes told her the woman didn't approve.

"I apologize if I kept you waiting," Savannah offered.

The dowager countess brushed her off by quickly making introductions. "Your Grace, may I present my son Roland's widow, Mrs. Savannah Dawson." She turned to Savannah. "Mrs. Dawson, may I present His Grace, Gabriel Armstrong, Duke of Clevedon. As you know, his Grace has graciously taken up the job of overseeing young Vincent's upbringing."

Savannah gazed into the angular, chiseled face of the duke. He was quite handsome, more than a man should be allowed. Never had she seen such a perfect specimen. If the duke knew how good-looking he was, he hid it well. Surely he must be used to being stared at by countless women in the ballrooms of London.

The duke took her gloved hand in his for a moment. "Mrs. Dawson. A pleasure to meet you, and my condolences on the loss of your husband. Roland was a close friend and will be missed, even if he was in America."

"Thank you, sir...Duke...Your Grace." Savannah

knew she was fumbling over her words, and the best thing she could do was say nothing.

She sat in a dark blue damask chair and held her breath for a moment, trying to regain her composure. Why was this man so alluring? Was it because of his title, or was it his beauty? She'd practiced all afternoon over how to speak to him, the man who would help her prepare Vincent for his role as earl. Now all she was doing was fumbling, and she knew her mother-in-law would be quick to point it out later.

"Vincent is quite excited to meet you, Your Grace. It's all he's talked about on our ride from London."

The duke glanced at the countess. He appeared uncomfortable about something.

"Vincent and the duke have already met. I had his governess bring him down from the nursery before he went to bed."

She tried not to act surprised, but by the narrowing of the duke's eyes, he recognized the dowager countess had caught her off guard. "He has? I would have liked to have said good night to my son."

The dowager countess raised her hand in a dismissive manner. "The boy can no longer be coddled."

"I fail to understand how my son saying good night to me is coddling him. Surely you must understand he's in a new house, surrounded by strangers."

"Perhaps I could accompany you to the nursery while we wait for dinner," the duke said.

It was an unusual request, but one Savannah hoped the dowager countess would not dismiss. Not in front of their guest. Lady Dorset nodded stiffly, "Very well, go ahead. I'll allow some leeway this time. But from here on out, Mrs. Dawson, you must agree to keep the boy on a schedule."

"He is my son, and I will not be told when I can or cannot see him."

She rose from her chair, nodded to the duke, and began to follow him. She knew she'd overstepped, but she would not be dismissed, nor would she be told when she would or would not be allowed to see her son. She certainly didn't need a duke to come between her and the dowager countess. She and her mother-in-law would have to learn how to coexist. Nevertheless, the duke, having clearly assessed the situation, had interceded on her behalf.

"I can't thank you enough, Your Grace, for doing this."

"Don't mention it. If we're going to see to young Vincent's education, we'll have to work together, else the dowager countess will take over."

"I know. Roland told me quite a bit about his mother, though I'm sure he never told me the entire story because he never expected any of this would have happened."

They began walking up the stairs to the third floor where the nursery was located. "Would you have stayed in America if Timothy hadn't been killed?" the duke asked.

"Probably. I had my family there, and they had been quite supportive until I got the news about Timothy."

"I take it they didn't approve of you uprooting the boy and bringing him to England?"

She smiled. "You would be right about that, Your Grace," she replied. "Tell me, how did a man of your stature become involved in helping raise a young boy who isn't even related to you?"

"Roland was a good friend. We'd known each other since we were very young boys. I would like to think he would have done the same for me if the situation were reversed."

He grasped the doorknob and began to open the door leading into the nursery.

"That would mean giving up a life in America," she said. She tried not to stare at him. He was one of the most handsome men she'd ever laid eyes on with his golden-brown hair that in the sunlight cast a hint of red. His emerald-green eyes were unlike any she'd seen before. A woman could melt under the gaze of those eyes. He was quite muscular from time spent outside, something she noted most of his peers didn't do.

"Touché, Mrs. Dawson."

Miss West, the governess, sitting by the fire reading a book, startled when they entered the room. "I'm afraid he's fast asleep."

"That's all right," Savannah said quietly. "I won't wake him. He's had a long, busy day."

Smiling, she entered Vincent's room and drew closer to the bed, bending down to give her young son a kiss and smooth his hair. When she straightened, she noticed the duke standing just outside the doorway. He watched her as though he were aware of the turmoil she must be going through.

She quietly closed the door and nodded to the duke. "Thank you."

He nodded and followed her out of the room. "Shall we rejoin Lady Dorset?"

"I suppose we must. Has she really always been like this?"

"Yes, always. Once she gets to know you, she'll warm up."

Savannah arched a brow. "You say that with some authority, Your Grace."

"I am well versed in how the dowager countess operates."

"Oh?"

"Yes. She's, well, complicated."

"That's being polite, Your Grace."

He stifled a laugh. "I suppose you're right."

As they approached the drawing room door, a footman opened it, and the duke followed Savannah inside. The dowager countess sat in the same spot she'd occupied when they'd left.

"Higgins has just announced dinner is ready." The dowager countess stood and walked toward the duke. He extended his arm to her. As the older woman placed her hand on his arm, he gazed over at Savannah, his full lips quirked up in amusement.

As per custom, the duke and countess led the way to the dining room. When they entered the room, there were three place settings at the far end. Trying to remember the protocol Roland had taught her, Savannah wondered if the duke would sit at the head of the table. There were too many rules to remember, and this was one of them. She was sure the dowager countess would remind her, and eventually, she would learn. As the mother of the earl, she had to.

Dinner wasn't quite as long and drawn out as Savannah had imagined. Her mother-in-law probably meant to keep it shorter for not only Savannah, but their guest as well. Savannah stayed quiet, not wanting to intrude on the conversation unless asked a question. She didn't want to give the countess any reason to publicly dress her down, as she seemed so fond of doing.

Savannah wondered if the two of them could ever be friends of some sort. For the time being, she was better off listening rather than adding too much to the conversation. Once the newness wore off and Vincent settled into a routine, she hoped the countess would back down and return to her own life. At least she could hope.

"If you have no plans for tomorrow, I thought you and Vincent could visit," the duke said suddenly. "I have a pony chosen for him, and he could begin riding lessons."

"That is most kind of you, Your Grace, but surely you don't have time to personally instruct Vincent."

"I won't be instructing him. Bart, one of my stable boys, will start out teaching him. I thought a younger boy rather than my stable master would better suit Vincent."

"It's very important Vincent learn to ride," Lady Dorset remarked. "The earlier he begins, the better, and I can't think of anyone more suited than the duke's staff."

Savannah nodded. "Very well, then. I'm sure Vincent will be excited. He loves horses."

She gazed discreetly at the duke out of the corner of her eye, watching him as he finished a lone piece of roast pheasant on his plate. She wasn't sure what to make of him. Certainly, he and Roland had been fast friends, but her late husband had shared little about his life in England. The stories he did relate were usually about his family, but even those were few and far between. Why agree to assist in raising his son? What would happen if she were to ever remarry? Would he continue on in his role, or would he allow her new husband to take over?

These were legitimate questions, which, for now, she'd keep to herself.

THE MOMENT she walked into the drawing room, Gabriel was intrigued by Savannah Dawson. He could easily see how she'd caught Roland's attention. She was beautiful with light-blonde hair and sapphire eyes, elegantly tall, and carried herself as though she were nobility. She wasn't pale in coloring like her English counterparts. The golden tone of her skin gave evidence of a love of the outdoors.

There was one thing about Mrs. Dawson that caused him pause. She was quite uninhibited in her manner of speaking. She said what was on her mind, though he was sure she still held back a great deal. Such a trait was not something one expected in a duchess. A duchess? He brushed the very thought away. Why would such an idea even cross his mind? She was his best friend's widow, and between them, things would always have to remain honorable and platonic.

Knowing the dowager countess, he was quite sure Mrs. Dawson's blunt manner offended her no end, as Mrs. Dawson had already shown she could stand up to her mother-in-law when it came to her son. Gabriel wondered how long it would be before she and the dowager countess had their first real falling-out.

She was truly unlike any woman he'd ever met, and this intrigued him. He needed to get a better understanding of this creature. He didn't want to offend her with his choices in how the boy should be raised. Vincent's status had changed the moment his uncle died, and Gabriel wasn't sure Mrs. Dawson understood that.

He wondered if Lady Dorset hoped to remove Mrs. Dawson from her son's life altogether so as to remove any uncouth American influence from her grandchild's life.

"Is everything all right, Your Grace?" he heard her trill.

He focused on Lady Dorset, hoping she hadn't caught him staring at the young woman.

"Yes, the meal is excellent as always," he replied smartly. He turned to Savannah. "What are American dinners like, Mrs. Dawson?"

She put her fork down on her plate and contemplated her answer. He wondered if she was merely attempting once again to be as polite as possible and not offend the countess.

"Roland and I had simple meals most of the time. The only time we might have something as fancy as this would be if we were invited to dine with someone of great influence, a politician, for example."

Gabriel caught the dowager countess eyeing her daughter-in-law in disbelief. "I would have assumed, given my son's station, he would have dined elaborately."

"No, ma'am, he preferred spending his evening dining with his wife and son."

"The boy was allowed to eat with you?" Not waiting for a reply, Lady Dorset carried on. "That is quite irregular, and I can assure you he won't be joining us every evening. Perhaps when he's older, but for now, he should spend his time in the nursery. Don't you agree, Your Grace?"

Fortunately for Gabriel, he didn't have to get in the middle of the discussion, because the boy's mother jerked her head around to face her mother-in-law.

"Vincent isn't a child you keep hidden away in the nursery. He's a young boy who's been through terrible trauma in his short life. He's lost his father and left the only place he's known. It is confusing, and if he wishes to dine with us rather than in the nursery, he will do so."

Savannah turned toward him. "I apologize for my outburst, Your Grace. You see I'm rather protective of my son. Especially right now."

He shook his head. "No need to apologize, Mrs. Dawson. You know far better than we how traumatic all this has been for young Vincent. Exactly why I suggested the pony and lessons. To occupy his mind with something else."

"Thank you, and I believe you're correct that keeping him occupied is a step in the right direction."

"Excellent. We'll begin with his riding lessons."

"His tutor will be arriving in the next day or two, so he'll have his studies to keep him busy as well," the dowager countess added. It was obvious she was not fond of someone speaking so frankly to her. This could prove to be quite interesting.

Savannah's shoulders noticeably tensed. "Who is this tutor, and what is he going to teach my son?"

"A Miss Augusta Smythe will tutor him in French and history. His nanny will see that he learns to read and write correctly," the countess replied.

"Vincent can already read and is quite proficient in his writing and reading skills for his age. He's a very eager student."

"In the ten minutes he visited earlier, I could tell he's a smart and curious young lad," Gabriel replied.

"Shall we retire to the drawing room? Brandy, Your Grace?" Lady Dorset asked.

"Of course. Then I must be on my way. I want to make sure I'm free to take Vincent to the stables to introduce him to his pony and instructor," Gabriel replied.

He stood and followed the ladies into the drawing room. He would make this fairly quick. Parr was waiting back at Brook Fall, and they had a chess game to play.

Gabriel enjoyed a brandy while the ladies had tea. Most of the conversation was light. He asked Mrs. Dawson about her early life growing up in America. He'd never been, and since history fascinated him, he enjoyed hearing from someone who had actually lived there. Gabriel understood many old English customs and traditions were honored there still.

Her father was a lawyer, which was how she and Roland had met. He'd been invited to dinner, similar to this evening, and before they knew it, Roland was calling on her. Gabriel caught a glimpse of the dowager countess, who was looking rather perturbed but keeping her opinions to herself. He wondered how much of his life Roland had really shared with her. From her pinched lips, he doubted she knew much.

He rose to take his leave. "I'll send my carriage around eleven for you and Vincent," Gabriel said, then addressed Lady Dorset. "You're welcome to come as well, Lady Dorset." He smiled.

"I'm afraid I won't be able to. I'm meeting with the vicar and a few of the ladies about autumn activities."

"Another time," he replied. Autumn was months away, and he wondered what she was really about. Certainly, it didn't take months to prepare for something so simple.

He bid his dinner companions good night and exited to his waiting carriage. He couldn't get Mrs. Dawson—Savannah—out of his mind the entire ride back to Brook Fall.

CHAPTER 4

*P*arr was waiting in his library for him when he returned. The chessboard was already set up, and he sat in front of it as though he were already contemplating his strategy.

"I was about to give up on you and retire for the evening," Parr said.

"It's not that late, and I believe I told you I had no intention to spend any more time there than I had to."

Parr picked up a crystal decanter. "Brandy?" he asked and began pouring into one of two snifters sitting next to the board. He sometimes irritated Gabriel with his familiarity and how he made himself at home.

Gabriel nodded, and removed his jacket and cravat. He sat down and studied the board and then Parr.

"Well, aren't you going to ask how I found the lady?" Gabriel growled.

"I presumed you would get around to it. Did you meet the boy as well?"

"Yes, and I thought it interesting how Lady Dorset handled this evening. She had the boy brought down while his mother was finishing getting ready."

"I imagine the mother was not happy about that," he replied.

Gabriel nodded and picked up his brandy. "No, she wasn't. In fact, I see a battle for control brewing between Mrs. Dawson and Lady Dorset."

"I hope she's up to a challenge, because I recall the countess has an acid tongue."

"I believe the lady can hold her own when it comes to Lady Dorset. I did, however, find something rather peculiar."

"What's that?" Parr asked before taking a swallow of brandy.

"I know Roland left to get away from his overbearing mother and egotistical brother. He tried to erase his ties to the nobility and had no interest in his family's estate."

"What's your point?"

"Lady Dorset clearly thinks less of her daughter-in-law because she is a commoner and an American." Gabriel shook his head and picked up a pawn. "No, the countess wants her daughter-in-law to fail."

"How could you deduce such an outcome from one simple dinner?"

"I know Lady Dorset and how she treated Roland. Timothy was always her favorite because she knew he would one day be earl. She never gave much affection or attention to Roland. He was a mere second son."

"Who, from what you've said, became a very wealthy second son in America."

"I'm sending my carriage for the boy and his mother in the morning. I've got a pony for the boy to learn on. I figured I would use the time wisely and try to get to know Mrs. Dawson better."

Parr barked out a laugh. "You've always been soft for a beautiful woman, which was my next question. How did you find her? Beautiful, ugly, or somewhere in between? You never said."

"She is beautiful, quite beautiful. She's also not afraid of speaking her mind."

"That's a definite mark against her," Parr snorted.

Gabriel moved his pawn. "Actually, I found it refreshing."

Best to leave it at that, or he'd have Parr questioning everything about the woman. He was relentless when it came to finding out information. So he turned the conversation to crops and how they were faring this year. He knew Parr had some of the best wheat crops around. He'd put all his money into this one crop, and it had paid off tenfold.

Gabriel, however, wasn't interested in crops and how much they did or did not profit. No, he found his thoughts wandering to Mrs. Dawson and how she intrigued him. Bloody hell, it was far more than intrigue. He found himself attracted to her, and that was most inconvenient.

CHAPTER 5

Savannah awoke to a flash of sunshine piercing the room as the maid opened the heavy drapes. She wasn't used to having someone wait on her like this. Most mornings, she got herself up and ready for her day. The lady's maid she did have in America had several tasks, one of them being helping Savannah with her clothing and, of course, tightening her corset. This was going to take some getting used to.

"Has my son had breakfast yet?"

"No, madam. He fussed, wanting to see you, so his governess called on me to awaken you so you could eat together. It usually isn't done, as the countess will tell you, but you and young Lord Dorset just arrived, and we saw no harm."

She rubbed her eyes and swung her legs over the side. "Thank you. Where will we be having breakfast, the nursery?"

"Yes, madam."

"Very well, let me dress. We're due at the duke's later this morning. I'll need to dress appropriately. He's to introduce Vincent to a pony and meet the stable boy who will be in charge of teaching him to ride."

"Your pale-yellow muslin is ready and would be quite appropriate."

Savannah shook her head. "No, we're going to the stables. The yellow will easily show dirt," she replied. "What about the brown print?"

"It is ready as well, madam."

A few moments later, she found herself on her way to the nursery. Her hair was tied back, and she wore a simple gray dress instead. The brown print made her appear too matronly. Yet, it didn't matter to her how she looked at the moment. Seeing Vincent was far more important. She wanted to see how he was adjusting to his new way of life, which meant things like not spending as much time with her as they had been and having a governess who would be helping to raise him, not that Savannah wouldn't keep herself apprised of everything that went on in Vincent's life.

"Mama!" he shouted, running across the room to her as she entered the nursery. "You came!"

She stooped to his level and hugged him. He was holding on to her neck so tightly, Savannah could scarcely breathe. "Come, let's eat breakfast. We have a busy morning."

"Yes, we are going to the Duke of Clevedon's estate to see his horses. I can't wait," Vincent said excitedly.

"It was very nice of the duke to invite us. You must remember to thank him before we leave," she reminded him.

"Oh, I will, Mama."

She sat at the small table to one side of the room. Breakfast had already been brought up. She began spooning eggs on both plates before adding sausage and toast as Vincent sat patiently waiting. Savannah was about to put a forkful of eggs into her mouth when her son spoke up.

"I don't like having to be here. There's no one for me to play with."

"I explained to you things would be different when we arrived. I also explained why. You must give it some time, Vincent," she replied. "I'm sure your opinion will change after today."

"Yes, ma'am." He appeared dejected, but began to eat his breakfast.

"We've talked about this. Many times. You can do this for Papa."

A couple of hours later, they were on their way to the duke's estate. It was a marvelous English day, the sky the bluest of blues, with puffy white clouds slowly moving along. It was perfect compared to some of the typical gray days they'd encountered already since their arrival.

The duke's estate ran alongside the Earl of Dorset's, making the ride a short one. Savannah marveled at the long drive lined with majestic oaks on either side that appeared as though they'd been there for generations. Beyond that lay lush rolling green hills enclosed on either side by the perimeter wall or smaller fencing to keep livestock enclosed. A couple of black horses lazily grazed, paying no mind to the approaching carriage.

Through it all, Vincent went from one side of the carriage to the other, gazing out at the majestic surroundings. It wasn't that Sky View wasn't just as magnificent, but the duke's estate was simply grander. Savannah quietly mused that if the drive was this beautiful, what must the rest of the gardens and even the house look like?

She didn't have long to wonder. As they made their way farther up the drive, a large structure appeared. She blinked twice when she realized this wasn't some mere manor house, but a castle, an actual castle. She closed her eyes again and opened them, trying to make sure they weren't playing a trick on her. They weren't.

Rather than stopping at a normal entrance, the carriage continued on through a large opening leading into a common area, a bailey by medieval terms. The carriage came to a stop in front of a massive oak door. Vincent jumped down as soon as the footman opened the door, the curiosity of a seven-year-old getting the best of him. Savannah sighed, deciding to allow her son some freedom to be a boy. His world was beginning to change, and she wanted to make sure the transition was smooth and painless. Soon he would be caught up in his book work and studies and would have time for nothing else. Which was as it should be for a young earl, but Savannah still held on to the belief that boys should be allowed to be boys.

Savannah descended from the carriage just as the door opened and an older gentleman appeared to greet them.

"Good afternoon, madam. If you would follow me..."

Vincent ran up to her, clearly excited by what he saw. "Mama, the duke lives in a real castle!"

"Yes, he does. Come, you can explore later. Right now, the duke is waiting."

Vincent carefully sized up the butler. "Good day, I'm Vincent Dawson, Earl of Dorset," he said with a hint of authority to his young voice.

"Good afternoon, Lord Dorset. It's very nice to make your acquaintance. I am Simmons, the duke's butler." He glanced at Savannah with a hint of a smile. "If you'll follow me."

They followed the butler into the darker interior. It took a moment for her eyes to adjust from the bright daylight. She gazed around in awe at the tapestries and portraits that hung on the walls. It was a completely different environment compared to Sky View. Unfortunately, she didn't have time to make further comparisons as the butler led them into a spacious drawing room done in shades of blue, dark blue being the predominant hue. There were landscape paintings, a couple of them reflecting the duke's obvious love of horses.

"I'll tell His Grace you've arrived," Simmons said, slipping out of the room.

Savannah found a blue-and-gold-damask chair to sit in and motioned to Vincent to do the same. She knew her son was having a hard time not being able to run around and explore everything. He was a very curious boy, always had been, but he came and climbed up onto a matching chair and sat quietly as he took in his surroundings.

They didn't have long to wait before the door swung open and the duke walked in. He wore buckskin-colored breeches, tall black boots, and a tweed jacket. His golden-brown hair was tousled from riding without a hat. If it were under any other circumstances, Savannah decided he might be the most perfect man she'd ever laid eyes on.

"Good morning," he said, nodding to each of them. "I hope you haven't waited long."

"Good morning, Your Grace, and no, we haven't had to wait," she replied, adding, "Your home is most interesting. I would have never imagined you lived in a castle."

A hint of a grin crossed his face. "The castle has been in my family for generations. Perhaps you'd like a tour after young Vincent is settled."

"I would enjoy that, Your Grace. Perhaps you can give me some history as we walk to your stables."

"Of course. I'd be happy to."

Vincent, who'd been quiet as a church mouse, finally broke his silence. "Can we go to the stables now, Your Grace?"

Savannah smiled, watching as Clevedon tried not to smile when he must have realized the young man was trying to be serious. "Yes, we can."

"Where are your stables?" Vincent asked eagerly.

"On the outside of the castle, housed in a separate building. They were built by my grandfather, who'd determined the castle would never be stormed by an enemy again. He decided the stables should be out on their own, for reasons you shall see."

He guided them back through the grand hall and outside. After crossing what he called a courtyard, they happened upon an oversized door. A footman opened the door, and they made their way onto the path leading up to the stables. The stables consisted of a long, white building, with various smaller paddocks and a gate leading into what Savannah surmised was a pasture.

"I noticed your two black Arabians out front," she said. "They're gorgeous."

"Thank you," he replied. "I'm using them as part of a new breeding program. They are known for their endurance, which, when crossed with an Irish thoroughbred, should make for a fine specimen."

She blinked and smiled. Men didn't normally go into details, especially about a subject most woman might find indelicate, but it was obvious the duke was passionate about his horses.

"Have you ever seen a Friesian or an Andalusian?"

"Yes, I saw Andalusians while I toured Spain some years back. The same with Friesians. They originated in an area of the Netherlands," he said. "Do you ride, Mrs. Dawson?"

"Yes, I loved to ride through our orchards," she said before changing the subject back to horses. "Have you ever seen a Palouse? They come from the West and were used by the Nez Perce Indians. They are quite nimble."

"I'm afraid I've never seen one up close. I've seen a few portraits at a gallery a few years back, but never in the flesh."

Vincent ran up to them, having been exploring along the path and having seen the stables as they neared them. It was farther away than Savannah had imagined, but as it came into view, she could see why. It was almost like a working farm on its own.

"Your stables are huge, Your Grace! How many horses do you have?" Savannah exclaimed.

"Quite a few," the duke said with a smile.

Satisfied with the answer, Vincent once again ran off in search of whatever it was little boys liked.

"He's a curious child. Smart too."

"He has been since the moment he learned to walk and was in leading strings."

The duke bent his head toward her. Savannah hadn't realized just how tall the man was until then. "How are you coping with turning over most of the boy's learning to others? I realize it's an entirely different lifestyle from what he's used to, so it can't be easy for you."

"May I be frank, Your Grace?"

"Of course, by all means."

"It would go easier if it weren't for the countess. She has an acid tongue and obviously a distaste for Americans. Or at least our way of life," she replied. "What I'm trying to say is that she isn't making it easy for me, but then it's only been a day, and we hardly know each other."

He nodded, listening closely. "Hopefully, she'll warm up once she gets to know you."

"One can hope."

They walked along the path in the early summer heat. Everything was perfect, at least for now. As they walked a little farther, the white-sided building housing the duke's stables came into full view. Once again Savannah felt as though she'd been transported to another time. Stables in America looked nothing like this.

~

GABRIEL GAZED down at the young woman walking next to him. She'd caught him completely off balance, especially this morning. He'd been sure she wouldn't be able to carry on a proper conversation with a peer since she'd been raised far away from the drawing rooms and ballrooms of England, yet she did it with a graceful ease, a breath of fresh air to him after all the encounters he'd had over the years with young debutantes and their mothers simply out to attract his attention for his title and wealth.

She enjoyed horses, and the two of them had an educated, detailed conversation about them, mainly about the various breeds both here and in America. The Palouse horse she described fascinated him. He'd certainly heard of them, and from what he'd read, he knew that Americans crossbred them with thoroughbreds or other horse breeds built for endurance depending on their needs. He'd never seen one in person as she had.

The short periods of time he'd spent in the company of her young son, Vincent, had also surprised him. Vincent reminded Gabriel of how he and his siblings acted when they were not in their father's presence, without a care in the world. Though Vincent had been slightly shy on their first meeting the day before, he quickly warmed up to Gabriel.

A young boy walked out into the sunlight leading

the dark bay pony Gabriel had found at Tattersalls on his last trip to London. He'd estimated Vincent should get several good years with his new mount, given the pony was larger. He'd had the animal outfitted with a saddle and bridle before having him brought to Brook Fall. Tommy White, son of his stable master, led the pony. He was about fifteen, and, given his age, the young man was a professional around horses, as his father had raised him to be. Tommy, like his father, had an uncanny connection to the beasts.

"Lord Dorset, this is Tommy. He'll be instructing you on this pony I found for you. Tommy, Lord Dorset."

"My pleasure, milord," he said, addressing Vincent.

"Is he mine?" he asked, looking up at Gabriel, and then the pony.

"Yes, he is. Now, why don't you follow Tommy. He'll take you to the paddock, and you can begin your first lesson."

He nodded and happily skipped beside Tommy and the pony as they turned to walk to a paddock used for training.

"He's beautiful, Your Grace. You really shouldn't have," Savannah said as she fondly watched her son.

"Every boy needs to learn how to ride and therefore should have his own pony."

Savannah nodded. She wasn't wearing a bonnet like most women would, and for a second, he imagined what the countess might say upon seeing Savannah outdoors in the direct sunlight.

"He's pestered me for a pony for the past two years, but I thought he was too young, and there wasn't anyone I felt comfortable with to teach him to ride."

"Young Tommy will be perfect for him. His father is my stable master, and the boy has been around the stables since he was out of leading strings."

He observed her as she enthusiastically watched her young son. Her full lips curved up into a smile, and her haunting blue eyes took everything in. "I have no doubt Vincent is going to flourish here. In the past two days he's been happier than I've seen him in a long time."

"Since his father died?" Gabriel inquired. "The countess has never really said much about Roland's death, so I'm afraid I'm at a disadvantage. The only thing I know is that his ship disappeared."

"Yes, his ship disappeared on a trip to a sugar plantation he had recently purchased. No sign of the ship was ever found, but the vessel never reached its destination."

"I understand storms can be quite wicked in that area."

"Yes, that's what Roland said once. The vessel belonged to his small fleet of cargo ships."

Gabriel shook his head as they stopped at the paddock fencing. "I'm sorry you had to go through that."

"Thank you, Your Grace. I finally had him declared dead by the courts after two years, once it was evident his ship had been lost at sea."

"Had something been found?"

"Yes. A piece of wood from one of the lifeboats. The plank of wood had the name of the ship on it," she replied. "That was sufficient enough for a judge, and my father thought it best I move on."

"Then of course Timothy's death occurred, and young Vincent became an earl overnight."

"Yes," she replied.

"Yes. Life has a strange way of turning out, doesn't it?" Gabriel said to no one in particular, but since Savannah was the only one standing near, the words were made for her ears.

She turned to him with a resolute smile. "Tell me something about you, Your Grace. I scarcely know much other than that you were Roland's friend and you're a duke. Do you have any brothers or sisters?"

Gabriel let out a laugh. "You know, then, that Roland and I went to school together, university too. I have a younger brother and two younger sisters. Henrietta is married to a Frenchman, and dangerous as it is they are living near Provence. Franny is visiting a friend who recently married and moved to Cambridge."

"What about your brother?"

"Charles is on his grand tour of the Continent at the moment."

"I understand that's quite a big event in a young man's life."

"It is. All young men should have one before they have to return home and begin their chosen professions."

"I take it you didn't have a grand tour, Your Grace?"

He cocked a brow in her direction. "Not at all."

She must have felt his unease. Gabriel wasn't used to sharing anything, much less business, with a woman. "Shall we watch young Vincent, or would you prefer to return to the house for tea?"

"I believe Vincent will concentrate better if I'm not watching, so I suppose it's tea, Your Grace."

He smiled down at her and offered Savannah his arm. They walked back toward the castle together. This woman had suddenly gotten him to open up about things he normally kept to himself. It was quite discomforting.

CHAPTER 6

Several days had passed since Savannah had seen the duke. They'd had tea while Vincent took his first riding lesson. While they waited for tea, Clevedon had shown her around the portrait gallery. It seemed they both shared an equal love of horses and history.

Vincent had been kept busy with his daily riding lessons and his schooling with a new tutor Lady Dorset had chosen. Not sure whether or not she liked the older man, Savannah decided to keep her thoughts to herself about Vincent's tutor until she had time to truly evaluate Miss Augusta Smythe.

Vincent, for his part, was settling in better than she'd imagined. He hadn't complained too much about his schoolwork. What he looked forward to the most was his horseback riding lesson. Without fail, each day, the duke would send a carriage or cart to fetch him.

Savannah was beginning to enjoy her new life. She had spent one day walking through the small village. The countess had a previous engagement, but had sent word ahead to a local modiste introducing Savannah and with instructions that she needed new dresses and accessories. She'd lost weight during the voyage over, and she hoped she could salvage a few of the gowns she'd brought along by having them altered and taken in. The countess, however, was having none of it, deeming what Savannah wore nowhere near the quality of what an English seamstress could create.

She'd also stopped at a shop and found a couple of pairs of kid gloves to replace her worn ones, and even found new threads for her embroidery, along with a new canvas. Though she found it disconcerting to wander about with no one else, Savannah had learned back when she received word of Roland's death that friends were few and far between. Now more than ever, she discovered just how alone she was. She hadn't met anyone, and the countess kept herself busy, making Savannah all the more determined to meet some of her local peers. Lady Dorset had talked about hosting a tea to introduce Savannah, but nothing had transpired.

This morning had changed all that when the duke sent around an invitation for her to ride with him. His note had said nothing else, just that he would be arriving for her late morning, and he would supply her with an appropriate mount.

In wanting to share the news with someone, she realized how utterly alone she was. Lady Dorset never arose before noon, and Savannah would be gone to ride with the duke by then. The dowager countess probably wouldn't have much good to say about the invitation, and Savannah was convinced nothing she did would meet with the woman's high standards.

She hadn't thought much of the life she'd left behind. It would do her no good, as there was nothing there for her. She needed to give it time. Things would fall in line. For now, she would dress for her ride and enjoy her time with the duke.

She thought of the tall, handsome man with the emerald-green eyes. Perhaps he might be able to give her some insight as to what her role and position were supposed to be now that her son was the earl. Lady Dorset had been of little assistance in this area. Whether it was because she thought Savannah should already know or if it was because she wanted her to fail, Savannah neither knew nor wanted to dwell on.

Abbott was in the middle of readying her riding outfit when Savannah entered the rooms where she stayed. It was hard for Savannah to get used to having her own lady's maid, as when she resided in America, when Roland had been alive, she did without. He was adamant about leaving his old life back at home in England. She wondered what he'd say now.

For her first time riding with the duke, she would be doing so sidesaddle, which, in her eyes, was dangerous and did nothing to help a woman truly enjoy riding. But she would do so, and without protest. It wasn't up to her to come in and make changes, ones that might not be welcome.

Her mind wandered back to the duke and to what he really thought on matters. Was he one who adhered to rigid rules, or was he more progressive and open-minded? Maybe their time together today would help her decide.

She took one last glimpse in the mirror at herself and the moss-green riding habit she wore. Of the two she owned, this one was the best, even though she'd had it for several years. Several years indeed, she mused. Since her husband's death, it had been difficult to keep up appearances. Although Roland had left both her and Vincent well provided for, her late husband's lawyer made it nearly impossible for her to spend anything. New clothing had been deemed frivolous. In the gentleman's mind, the money was there for when Vincent became of age. Until then, the two of them were to live as modestly as possible.

"The duke's carriage just arrived, madam," Abbott proclaimed as she reentered the room. Savannah had her thoughts about the plain young woman, but now was hardly the time.

"Thank you, Abbott," she replied, adding, "I'm not sure what plans the countess has, if any, for tonight, but please make sure the rose-colored gown is ready."

A few minutes later, she ascended into the elegant black lacquered coach and sat back against the richly appointed black leather seats. The duke had mentioned in a discussion with her his love of horses, and that same adoration was evident in his luxurious carriage. The coach was pulled by two matching white horses. She smiled, recalling how when he'd sent for her and Vincent, the carriage had been pulled by two matching blacks. Horses were definitely a passion of Clevedon's.

A few minutes later, the coach pulled up at the front door of the castle. The duke himself was there to greet her, standing near two horses, which were held by stable boys. One was obviously the duke's personal mount, a black stallion, pawing the ground, anxious to run. Nearby, a gray horse stood quietly.

"Good day, Mrs. Dawson. I hope this ride will serve as a good diversion."

"It's a perfect day, Your Grace." Clevedon was dashing in his buckskin breeches and brown boots. He wore a dark tweed jacket over a crisp white shirt and cravat. She felt her heart quicken as he took her hand.

He led her toward a mounting block while the young groom readied her horse. "I chose Matilda for you because you're an experienced rider, and she's quite adaptable to any situation."

"She's beautiful, and thank you for not putting me on an older, docile animal."

Once she had mounted, he nodded and swung his

leg over the back of his stallion, who was having to be held by a groom.

"Come, I thought you might like to see where we are clearing for the railway to cross."

"I hope the noise won't be too much to bear, Your Grace."

"Not at all. It's at the far end of my property, well away from the house."

She smiled warmly. "Don't you mean castle?"

"I take it you've never seen a castle until you came to England?" he asked, bringing his horse nearer.

"As you're well aware, Your Grace, we don't have castles in America."

"Pity."

"Come now, Your Grace. America isn't that old. Your home is at least, what, two hundred years old?"

He laughed, his deep rich baritone rumbling from his chest. "Try six hundred, and through it all, it's been inhabited by the Armstrong family."

After a short gallop across a meadow, they walked their horses, letting both animals rest a bit. Savannah was amazed at the lushness of the landscape. She gazed across at the duke, who gazed toward a stone wall that ran along one side of the field. "I understand from Lady Dorset that your business ventures are many. Far beyond the estate."

"Lady Dorset would be correct. In these days and times, one must expand one's interests. With industrialization, one cannot rely on farming as was done in the past."

"Roland thought the same thing."

"Which was why he had a small fleet of ships to carry cargo. I understand some of his ships were steam powered."

Savannah nodded. He'd obviously done his research. "Yes, he had expanded more into the steam-powered ships. As I mentioned, he was aboard one when he disappeared at sea."

She sensed he was uncomfortable talking about how Roland died, as he quickly changed the subject. "Have you seen the townhome in London the family keeps?"

"The countess has mentioned it, along with the fact that I desperately needed to visit her modiste there for more fashionable clothes. Not that the woman in the village isn't capable."

"I'm sure the village women are quite capable, but the dowager countess insists on the best, as I'm sure you're learning," he replied. "London has a wonderful culture. Have you been to the theater before?"

"No, I've never attended. Roland said it reminded him too much of the stuffiness of home."

Gabriel barked out a laugh. "That sounds like something he would say."

She smiled. "It does, doesn't it?"

"We need to remedy that," he said, gazing over at her.

"What are you talking about, Your Grace?"

"I have business in London. I was thinking perhaps you could find a reason to make the trip as well. I'm sure Lady Dorset would love any excuse to return to Town."

"We could do that, I suppose. Are you interested in taking me to the theater, Your Grace?"

"Yes, and showing you around London."

A thrill shot through her at the prospect, which she tried to temper with practicality. "What about Vincent? I can't take him with me, away from his studies."

He arched a brow. "Part of being the mother of such a young earl is that you can leave him with the knowledge he'll be safe and well taken care of. You have competent people looking after him and teaching him. No reason to sit at home all the time."

Savannah really wanted to spend time with this handsome man, but she was overwhelmed by all the emotions she felt. Dare she accept his invitation? To spend an evening at the theater accompanied by the duke himself...it was the stuff dreams were made of. Her heart beat faster as she considered accepting, but then she remembered who she was, and what her responsibilities were. She bit her lip and tore her gaze from his. "I couldn't possibly, Your Grace."

"But you must. Trust me on this."

She gave him a small smile. "Very well. I'll at least give it some thought."

"That's all I ask. Now, would you care to take a run to that rowan tree at the top of the hill?"

That was all it took. Savannah dug her heel into the mare's side, and the pair began galloping up the grassy incline. She turned to catch a glimpse of the duke. He was obviously holding his stallion back. The mare was quick, but no match for the duke's horse.

For a moment, she thought he was going to allow her to beat him to the tree, but she was mistaken. A flash of black passed her, the duke grinning madly as he made a dash for the rowan. Savannah followed, knowing she had not a chance of gaining on the duke and his black beast.

She pulled up alongside him. The view was breathtaking on this perfect English day with the large meadow spread out all around them, the lush green grass blowing softly in the breeze. There wasn't a cloud to be seen and the sky a light blue.

"It's beyond beautiful, Your Grace. If this hill were on Sky View, I would spend much time up here under this beautiful old tree."

He startled her with his answer. "You are welcome anytime."

She smiled shyly and glanced away from him. It was then that she noticed a tall round tower off to her left. It was intriguing, sitting on top of a hill, gazing at everything around it. Savannah wanted a better view.

"What is that structure?" she asked.

"A tower one of my great-grandfathers built. Would you care to see it?"

"Yes, if you don't mind."

He shook his head of golden hair, the back hanging just below his collar. "Not at all." He gently urged his horse into a walk, and she fell in beside him. When they came upon the structure, she stared up at it in awe. Three turrets graced the top of the round tower.

"One of my great-grandfathers was slightly eccentric. He had this built as a lookout. Men posted here could see for miles, so if anyone was coming, they could warn the duke of impending visitors."

"Was he afraid of being attacked?"

"Yes, and the tower gave him an advantage."

She smiled. "It appears quite large. Was it lived in? I'd love to see inside."

"Yes. Unfortunately, it is locked. I'll bring the key another time. As you can see, there's a circular staircase that winds all the way to the roof, which is where the men would hold watch."

"The view is spectacular, I imagine."

He nodded, smiling. "It is. My brother and I used to play here, even though we were not allowed."

"Why were you not allowed?"

"Our father probably thought we might fall from the roof. Once, after he caught us, he installed a new lock on the door and told us we were forbidden to play there."

She giggled. "Somehow, I doubt either of you listened to your father's mandate."

He arched a brow and smiled. "You would be correct, madam."

They continued their ride in relative quiet. Savannah was ashamed of herself for being attracted to the duke. It had been over two years since Roland had been lost, yet she still at times thought she owed him more than the year of mourning. Riding beside Clevedon made her push all that to the back of her mind and enjoy the present. He was easy to talk to, at least when one got him away from the stuffiness of his duties.

He brought his stallion to a halt and pointed to the sky, where a bank of dark, almost black clouds appeared. "I'm afraid we're going to have another storm. We need to return to the house before the rain sets in. I'll show you the rest another time."

"Very well, though I believe it's rained more than I've seen the sun since we arrived."

"It only seems that way, I can assure you."

They made it back to the castle minutes before a slow, methodical drizzle set in. Savannah let the duke assist her from the mare and lead her inside.

"Tea?" he inquired as he stopped before a massive oak door.

"Yes, please," she replied.

A footman opened the door just as the butler appeared. The duke spoke low to the man and continued to follow her inside. This was a different room, done in shades of red with gold accents throughout. It was as elegant as any drawing room she'd seen in her short time in England, the only drawback being that there was no access to the outside except for windows.

"This is lovely," she remarked as she sat down on a gold upholstered couch.

"It's my favorite public room because of the lighting."

"I can see why, but don't you miss having access to a garden?"

He smiled faintly. "You can't miss what you don't have."

A shiver of desire went through Savannah's body as she listened to his rich, deep baritone. She could never remember Roland's voice doing that sort of thing to her, but the duke was different. His voice fit his handsome good looks. She realized she'd reached a decision about him.

She should like to get to know him better.

"Has the dowager countess mentioned the soiree she and Lady Margaret hold every summer?" he asked as the two of them enjoyed tea while the rain pattered outside.

"Yes. It's all she can speak of. She and Lady Margaret meet several times a week to go over one or more aspects of throwing such a lavish party."

"I can only imagine."

"She told me just last night how coveted invitations to the ball were because such a small number of people were invited."

He nodded and put his cup down on the table before him. "It is one of the summer's highlights," he politely replied.

"I haven't seen a guest list, but I'm sure you must be on it."

"I can attest I've received an invitation. Rather than decline, I make it a point to go and spend no more than an hour at it. That seems to please both her and Lady Margaret."

"I've yet to have the pleasure of meeting Lady Margaret. They've been meeting at her house."

He felt himself smile, something he didn't normally

do. "Consider yourself lucky. She and the countess are like two peas in a pod."

"Probably because they've known each other since they were young girls," she offered.

"How did you know that?"

"Because Lady Dorset can talk endlessly of when they were young girls, before they married and had children of their own. It's as if the two of them were the only young ladies here in the country."

He laughed. "For being here such a short amount of time, you certainly know the countess."

"Roland told me all about her."

"Yes, I'm sure he did."

This was an awkward subject matter to discuss. He'd heard rumors about his friend, ones that didn't paint him in a favorable light. Until he had proof, he would say nothing. She fascinated him. Though he usually didn't find himself drawn to outspoken women, he found this one to be a breath of fresh air. He'd thought that the moment he'd first met her.

"I enjoyed our ride, Your Grace."

"Next time, we'll ride across Sky View. It would be good for you to learn your way around the estate."

She nodded. "I still want to look out from your tower, Your Grace."

He barked out a laugh. "We'll do that as well."

Setting her teacup on the table, she smiled. "I'm sure you have more pressing matters than me. I should let you get back to them."

"I've enjoyed your company, Mrs. Dawson."

"As I have yours."

He rose from his chair, setting his teacup down. "Let me see to the carriage."

Gabriel left in search of the butler. He didn't have to go far, as Simmons was speaking with a footman. The butler dismissed the footman and walked closer. "Your Grace?"

"See that the carriage is brought around. Mrs. Dawson is ready to leave."

"Yes, Your Grace. Is there anything else?"

"No, that'll be all."

He turned to walk back into the library. He normally wouldn't have a young woman at the house, but Mrs. Dawson was a widow, thus making it possible for her to do things her unmarried counterparts couldn't. Then again, she was American, and the rules of English aristocracy didn't apply. Or so Mrs. Dawson thought.

Yes, indeed. She was quite interesting. He desired to get to know her better, but was unsure how he wanted to pursue their friendship. They were brought together by her son, and their lives would intermingle for many years to come. Did he simply want to be her son's protector, or did he want to pursue more with the boy's mother? He was torn, which was not like him.

He returned to the drawing room, where he found Savannah thumbing through a book of sonnets he'd left on a table. Gabriel found her to be quite lovely, even graceful. He inhaled as he tried to get his emotions under control.

CHAPTER 7

The day of Lady Dorset's soiree finally came. Though it was being held at Lady Margaret's estate, Sky View was quite under siege, especially in the kitchen with the cooks frantically baking cakes and other sweets for the buffet. Savannah had managed to stay well out of the line of fire. Though she wanted to learn the British way of hosting such affairs, for once she was thankful she was American and that the countess had a distaste for them.

She hadn't seen the duke except from afar when he personally brought Vincent back after his riding lessons. Her son adored the duke, but Savannah herself was unsure of how she felt about the man.

One moment, her heart melted. Emotions that made her feel as though she were betraying Roland. The next minute, she cursed herself for even carrying on a personal conversation with the duke. She was just a common American who would be ridiculous to set her sights on a duke and getting her hopes up would only result in getting her heart broken and Vincent's relationship with the duke being jeopardized.

She made a vow to herself to stay away from him at all costs except for having to deal with him regarding

Vincent. Then there were the other times, like riding with him. She couldn't very well refuse him, at least not too many times, or it would seem rude. She simply couldn't trust her feelings, and that unnerved her.

Sitting on a window seat in her rooms, Savannah glanced down into the gardens. They were one of the things she'd come to love about England. She thought back to Roland and how he tried to duplicate an English garden, but had miserably failed due to the fact he was not a gardener in any sense of the word. He was too proud to hire a man to do it, so what few gardens their house had were small, planted and maintained by Savannah.

Roland had always been busy. His shipping and railroad interests had taken off, and he even expanded to England, though he had a man to handle the affairs back on English soil. She'd often wondered why he'd gone to the Caribbean that fateful voyage. He seldom if ever traveled by ship, having experienced a couple of bad voyages, which was what made it so hard to accept his death.

Once this affair was over, she needed to go to London and meet with Roland's man of business and see where matters stood. Which brought her to another conundrum. She needed someone who was well-versed in business to accompany her in order to make sure she wasn't being taken advantage of. Unfortunately, the only man who came to mind was the duke, but he would be the best choice, and she knew he wouldn't refuse her. Vincent's future interests were at stake, and even if the businesses were sold off, the duke would make sure she got a fair price, or he would make sure they were run correctly.

Savannah was pulled out of her thoughts by her lady's maid. She could hear the young woman in the background as she got Savannah's things in order.

"I have a bath drawn, madam," Abbott said before disappearing from sight.

"Thank you, Norma," Savannah called out after her. Though the countess had reprimanded her for using the woman's Christian name, Savannah could not bear the thought of addressing her maid with such disregard.

Savannah walked to the dressing room, where she allowed Norma to help her undress. She noted the sapphire-blue gown she was to wear laid out neatly. Never had she worn anything quite so elaborate, but as the countess had reminded her, she was the mother of an earl. Meaning expectations had changed. The local modiste had sewn the dress, as there had been no time to go to London. London would wait until the next week. Lady Dorset had already written her modiste and made an appointment for Savannah to be fitted with an entire new wardrobe. It would be the first time she'd ever been fitted by someone trained in France.

She wanted to soak longer in the tub, but Norma fussed at her, saying they were running behind and that the countess did not like tardiness, so instead, she got out, dried herself off, and went to stand by the hearth while Norma assisted her.

Finally, she gazed at herself in the mirror. She had to admit the gown was breathtaking and would make an unforgettable impression. The bodice was cut in such a way that more cleavage than she was used to baring showed. With her jewelry collection being small and understated, Savannah chose a pearl choker to wear. It was the best she could do until she went to London. She was pleased and made sure to thank Norma for her efforts.

She made her way downstairs, where the countess was waiting for her in the drawing room. One look at her pinched lips, and Savannah knew she was tardy, at least in the countess's eyes. She had meant to visit with Vincent before she left, but time had gotten away from her, and the countess would not tolerate waiting on Savannah while she went to the nursery.

Instead, when Savannah entered the drawing room, the countess rose from a dark blue damask chair and came toward her. She stopped momentarily to study Savannah up and down before breezing past her. "Come, we must leave now. Lady Margaret was expecting us to already be there."

"My apologies for my tardiness."

"Too late for apologies now. We need to be on our way."

She followed the countess out of the drawing room and outside to where the carriage awaited them. Ascending after the countess, Savannah took the rear-facing seat in order to give the countess more room. She knew the countess wasn't one for small talk, especially with her, so Savannah sat with her hands folded on her lap.

The pair rode in silence the short distance to Lady Margaret's estate. Again Savannah was amazed at all the detail. A large fountain laid claim to the center of the entrance. Carriages had to stop in front of it at the front door.

Candles were lit in every window, making the house seem almost magical. As they neared the tall, dark wood double doors, torches blazed from their holders.

They entered the house, where Lady Margaret and her husband stood in a reception line. They were announced by a very old, stodgy butler. Lady Dorset took her place beside her dear friend. As Savannah attempted to follow the countess's lead, she was dismissed by Lady Dorset. The gesture caught Savannah off guard, as it was a deliberate swipe at her.

"Go on to the ballroom," the dowager countess said. "I'm sure you can manage on your own."

"Yes, my lady. I'll be quite fine," Savannah replied before turning to walk across the room along with fellow partygoers. She would be damned if she'd allow the woman to upset her.

Savannah saw no one else she really knew, but noted some of the faces were vaguely familiar. Then she noticed the Duke of Clevedon standing across the room, talking with a small group of ladies. If he'd seen her, he didn't let on. No, she mused, he hadn't seen her. He was too busy making idle conversation with the giggling young women to notice her.

She had no reason to expect anything from him. Though she understood he made a habit to watch Vincent ride during his lessons, the duke had not invited her riding again and was having no problem avoiding her. Why did she let him get under her skin? She needed to stay away from this man. She would never be elevated enough to move in his social circles. She would be polite this evening, but she wasn't going to be fooled by his charm.

Another gentleman approached the small group. Savannah was unsure who the man was as she knew almost no one, and her mother-in-law had made no effort to try to introduce her to anyone. That was what this evening was supposed to be about, but Savannah felt as though the countess was doing her best to make her feel unwelcome. Perhaps with time, the older woman would mellow. She surely loved her grandson, Vincent, who made her eyes light up whenever he was around. It had to be because Vincent favored his late father in so many ways. He certainly looked more like his father than her, and some of his mannerisms were the same as Roland's. It was almost as though a younger version of Roland were present, and that seemed to bring the countess great comfort. Even a woman with an acid tongue would melt.

She skirted the perimeter of the ballroom. It wasn't a large crowd, but not knowing anyone made being on her own all the more painful.

"Good evening, Mrs. Dawson. I thought the countess would have you busy and not leave you alone acting like a scared doe." The familiar voice of the duke caught her off guard, and she was afraid it showed. There were plenty of young ladies and their mothers vying for his attention, why must he seek her out.

"Good evening, Your Grace," she replied. She studied the tile floor as she desperately tried not to peer into his eyes. She was unable to hide her feelings and any eye contact would immediately give away her most intimate thoughts. "The countess is busy with Lady Margaret, and I'm hardly anything like a scared doe."

"Really, the way you gaze upon everyone with fear makes me wonder if you aren't a terrified young deer."

He was comparing her to a deer? Still? How annoying could he be? Obviously, this was solely her opinion, as all the other young women seemed in awe. Of course, they were attempting to catch his attention. Clevedon, however, appeared unfazed by any of his feminine followers.

His gaze shifted downward to the empty dance card on her wrist. "I can hardly believe your dance card isn't full," he said reaching toward it. "Here, allow me to take two dances."

"It's empty because I know no one. Besides, who wants to dance with a matron?"

"I do."

She tried not to stare at him as he stood before her in a black suit, with a crisp white shirt and cravat. The jacket and trousers fit him perfectly, obviously he had one of London's finest tailors at his disposal. His golden-brown hair hung just at the collar, and he was freshly shaved. It ought to be a sin for a man to be so handsome. "Your Grace, please don't pity me."

"Pity you? Hardly."

She arched a brow. "Don't you like to dance?"

"Not particularly, but I do make exceptions, and besides, I want to dance with you."

"Because I have no mother hovering near me who has great expectations of marrying her daughter off to a duke?"

He cocked her a grin. "I always knew you were an intelligent woman, Mrs. Dawson." He passed her dance card back to her. "We have the next waltz, and another one later, if that meets with your approval."

"Pretty sure of yourself for a man who doesn't dance."

"I can assure you I dance decently, though I'm not as good at some of the livelier ones."

"I find that hard to believe, Your Grace." Savannah shook her head. "Aren't you afraid what people might say? Besides, I'm sure you have more important things to do, like visit your friends in the cardroom."

"I don't care about what other people think, and I cannot abide you being by yourself. At least allow me to introduce you to some of guests."

"Very well. If you're sure, Your Grace."

"Of course I'm sure. I cannot leave you alone. It isn't proper."

Savannah walked alongside the duke as he introduced her to people. They respected him, though she was sure part of that was because he was a duke. That alone commanded respect. She imagined most had known him since he was a boy.

The music started up for another set, and the duke led her onto the dance floor. "I believe this is my dance," he said, gathering her in his arms. A rush of feelings came over her as she placed her hand in his and the other on his shoulder. "Don't worry, I won't bite." He granted her a smile before leading her around the room.

Couples swirled by. Everything and everyone were a blur to her, all but the duke. Out of the corner of her eye, she could see young women and their mothers watching the two of them with interest. Then the outline of Lady Dorset came into her line of sight. Savannah could tell she was displeased by the way she pursed her lips in disdain.

"Oh dear, the countess doesn't seem at all happy we're dancing," she moaned.

"She has no reason to be displeased. If she'd introduced you properly, you might be dancing with another man. I can't imagine why she would be unhappy I've chosen to dance with you, being as I usually only dance one or two times at any given soiree."

"Perhaps she doesn't want you to feel obligated. I know I don't. You're doing enough overseeing Vincent and his education."

He smiled. "He's come a long way. Vincent's a very likeable young man. I foresee him doing quite well for himself in the future. The earldom will thrive with him."

"You are too kind, Your Grace," she replied. She blushed at his comments. It had been a long time since anyone had said anything positive about her or her son. Not even the countess would crack her tough exterior for a compliment or kind word.

"My pleasure, and enough with the Your Graces. I get that enough from everyone else. So much so, I sometimes feel like I've turned into my father."

She giggled. "You have, in a way."

"What?"

"You have turned into your father. At least as far as being the duke. As the man, I wouldn't know, since I never knew your father."

The dance was unfortunately coming to an end, and Savannah didn't want it to. She wanted, at this moment, for everything to continue as it was. Tonight, she felt like she was in a fairy tale, but what sort of ending would it have? Right now, this minute, he was caring and interested in what she had to say.

He reluctantly led her off the dance floor. She had just agreed to take refreshment with him when the countess approached.

She tsked quietly so as not to be heard. "My dear, you mustn't monopolize all the duke's time."

"I can assure you, madam, that my time has not been monopolized by your daughter-in-law. I find her charming and delightful."

His compliments made her blush once again.

"You are too kind, Your Grace, but I know Lord Simpson was searching for you. Something about racehorses I'm sure," the dowager countess said.

"Thank you. I'll be sure to find him as soon as I know Mrs. Dawson is comfortable."

The dowager countess had no alternative but to remain silent and nod as he led Savannah toward the refreshment table.

"The woman has no boundaries," he muttered.

"No, she doesn't."

He found a passing footman and took two glasses of lemonade. "If I didn't know she would reprimand you later, I'd ask you to go for a walk in the gardens."

"I'm not a child, Your Grace...Gabriel. If I want to take a turn in the garden with you, I will." She addressed him with a cheeky smile.

"You will?" he asked, startled.

"Yes. I'm in no need of a chaperone. I can go where I want, with whom I want."

She could tell by his grin that this not only pleased him, but it caught him off guard. She spoke her mind, always had. It was a trait she'd tried to keep under control while Roland was alive. Now, as a young widow with a child, if she didn't speak up for herself, who would?

~

"CLEVEDON? You haven't heard a word I've said, have you?" Viscount Long chuckled. He raised a glass of brandy to his lips. "Whoever she is, you're obviously quite taken with her."

Long was a portly man. His hair was thinning, and his face was a mottled red from too much drink. He and Gabriel had known each other since university, but time had done its damage to Long far too soon. No longer was he the spry, muscular young man Gabriel had once known. Instead, Long had gotten caught up in politics, waiting for the day he would take his place in Parliament. Until his father died, Long was stuck on the sidelines, which didn't bode well for him.

"Sorry to disappoint you," Gabriel replied. "My thoughts were with another shipment from the Caribbean being lost at sea."

"What of it? It's not the first time, nor will it be the last. Or did you have an interest in the ship?" Henry Littleton asked. The man had become the fifth Duke of Dover when his father had suddenly died from an apoplexy nearly two years ago. Unlike other sons who took on their father's places in Parliament and echoed their late sire's political views, Littleton was the complete opposite.

"I had no interest in the ship personally. I merely

find it interesting that this has become an ongoing problem."

"Storms happen, ships are lost," Long said.

Gabriel arched a brow and took a sip of brandy. "This is true. What I find unsettling is that they have all been ships that have left the same island."

"What are you thinking, Clevedon? Pirates?" Long muttered.

"It wouldn't be the first time," Gabriel replied.

Gabriel had done some digging into Roland Dawson's business dealings since becoming young Vincent's protector. The family owned a plantation on that very same island from which the missing ships had left. He found that even without Roland, the plantation thrived. Of course, most did, the English owners traveling to their holdings perhaps once a year. Roland had certainly done that more than once, the evidence showed.

A nagging feeling tugged at Gabriel. He couldn't shake it. As Lady Dorset had asked him to escort her daughter-in-law to visit the family solicitors, Gabriel was already devising a plan to discreetly ask the right questions. No solicitor would question him. He was merely looking after the interests of the widow and her son, who just so happened to be the current earl.

Until he escorted Mrs. Dawson to London, he could only sit back, listen, and watch, and, most importantly, keep his opinions to himself.

Dover downed his brandy, then set the glass on a table next to where the trio was standing. "I apologize, gentlemen, I must find my lady wife. I promised her a dance or two."

"By all means. You certainly can't anger your wife." Long chuckled.

"No, and if I did, she wouldn't speak to me for who knows how long."

Dover nodded. "Wives are not to be coddled. It

opens the door too far to them having their own opinions."

"Are you speaking from experience?" Gabriel inquired.

"But of course. Now, if you will excuse me."

"See what you're missing by not being married?" Long grunted after their friend left.

"Why marry at all if you're going to constantly complain about your wife?"

"Because we all need heirs. You should know that better than most."

"I'll not be forced into a loveless marriage, arranged or not. Besides, Charles is my heir right now."

"A brother doesn't count," Long replied. "A son is the future."

"If and when the occasion arises, I'll marry. Until then, I won't be dragged kicking and screaming to the altar."

"Still blaming Marie?"

Lady Marie, the one woman who had been able to capture his attention. He'd made such a fool of himself, only because her own father was a duke and Gabriel had been young, ambitious, and foolish. He had courted her shamelessly, like a puppy. Her father and his agreed to the match, and a spectacular wedding had been planned.

That wedding had turned out to be disastrous. Unbeknownst to Gabriel or anyone else, including her own father, Lady Marie had a tendre for the second son of the Earl of Southampton. Rather than end their betrothal with Gabriel privately before the wedding, Lady Marie had chosen to leave him at the altar.

He'd stood there until finally, Milford Parr found out the bride would not be arriving and that she had disappeared, leaving behind her wedding dress, a tearful maid, and a score of unanswered questions while she and her lover made their way toward Gretna Green.

Heartbroken, Gabriel swore at the time he'd never marry.

Until now. He had loved Marie, but was left heartbroken and humiliated by what she did to him. To them. Running off with another man—something he never saw coming. He was conflicted by his growing feelings for Savannah. He was falling desperately in love with her.

CHAPTER 8

Savannah was excited to go to London. Unfortunately, the weather had turned against them, the rain from the summer storms making for a longer than usual ride. Besides the weather, she had to endure the journey with Lady Dorset. Her mother-in-law had been displeased by Savannah's entry into English society. What the woman expected, Savannah was unsure, but she had a feeling the countess would make sure she was aware of every mistake she'd made.

She sat across from the dowager countess and took out a book she'd brought along with her, hoping not only to get some reading done, but to use the book as a diversion. The last thing she wanted was to spend the time engaged in conversation about what she'd done wrong and how her mother-in-law intended to fix it.

Vincent had not been allowed to accompany them, as the countess insisted the boy didn't need to be taken from his studies. Savannah had tried to explain to her that her son could easily be taught in London by his tutor and governess. London, she'd said, would be a perfect backdrop. Vincent's governess could take him to museums and landmarks he'd never seen. However, her ideas fell on deaf ears. Lady Dorset was having none of it.

Savannah's thoughts wandered to the duke. Rather than accompany the two women, he'd made his excuses citing business meetings. Savannah silently agreed with him, knowing his meetings were merely excuses to avoid riding to London with two women.

The duke had been quite attentive, especially at the ball. He made an effort to introduce her to people he thought important, which was more than the countess had done. They had danced twice, both waltzes. Though he insisted he was a horrid dancer, Savannah found the duke to be light on his feet as he guided her around the dance floor.

He was, however, the exact opposite from any man she might have chosen. Her reasons had not changed. Or had they? She felt herself drawn to this man for all the wrong reasons. This attraction was impossible. It could never happen. A relationship between a duke and an American commoner would never be accepted by his peers. Also, while many women in similar situations might look to a man for protection, outside of Vincent, Savannah didn't want or need one. Once she learned how to navigate English society, she would be able to fend for herself. If she needed the duke's assistance with business or Vincent, she would call on him.

The silence was suddenly broken by the dowager countess. "When we arrive in London, you may sit with me, and I'll explain why we're either accepting or denying an invitation. It will help you learn about proper English society and how things work, as I'm sure there was no culture or custom in America."

"I would like that as I find society here a bit over-whelming. Your assistance is most appreciated," she said with feigned gratitude.

The countess gave her a smug smile. "I have

arranged an appointment for tomorrow with my modiste in London. I told her you would need gowns for the evening, day dresses, riding habits, undergarments. Everything."

"That is most generous of you."

Lady Dorset lifted her hand as though to dismiss her compliment. "You were married to my son and are mother to the earl. You must look and act the part, even if you are American."

Savannah arched a brow. "Why do you have such a distaste for Americans?"

"Most Americans have snubbed our ways, only to attempt to reclaim them if the need arises. So many Americans aren't from old family money. They're new money and know very little about the ins and out of proper living."

"I'm sure your insight will be most useful," she replied with forced pleasantness.

"You're still young enough that the idea of another marriage shouldn't be completely dismissed."

"I'm not interested in marriage. I have all I need with Vincent. Besides, considering my son's now an earl, I'm afraid I'll be used as a means to get to him and his fortune. I won't allow that."

Smiling, the countess said, "You pleasantly surprise me, my dear. Most women in your position would never imagine a man would take advantage of them like that."

"I've heard of it happening far too many times, and I don't intend to fall victim. If I should ever meet a man I would consider marrying, of course."

"Of course," the dowager countess replied. "Luckily for you, you have me and the duke to guide you should the need arise."

"The duke has far more important matters than overseeing me."

"I've seen the way he looks at you, my dear."

"You must be mistaken. The duke and I are ill-suited."

Lady Dorset smiled and sat back again. "Don't believe for a moment he would be interested in a foreign commoner. Better to set your sights lower, my dear."

She needed to change the subject. "Did you know His Grace's parents?" Savannah asked.

"Of course I knew them," she replied. "Now there was a couple in love, in spite of their match being arranged."

"They were?"

"Oh yes. I've never seen such a devoted couple. The old duke was devastated beyond consoling when he lost his wife. I swear her death was the end of him. He was never the same after she died."

"What about you and the earl? Was it an arranged marriage as well?"

"Yes, our union had been arranged from the time we were born. There was never any doubt we would marry."

Savannah was quite surprised that the countess had opened up, even if she already knew the answer. Roland had told her years ago of how his parents had been paired. It was quite different hearing it directly from her mother-in-law.

"Women are nothing but merchandise when it comes to an arranged marriage," Savannah said. "She is a pawn in both families' desire to better themselves, no matter what the cause."

Shockingly, the countess agreed. "You are correct. Unfortunately, that is the way of the world."

"I'm grateful to have met Roland. Our marriage was based on love and trust."

"All the more reason to beware of fortune seekers now."

Savannah sighed. "That's what I'm afraid of."

The countess wiggled her way to the corner of her seat and made herself comfortable. "You're smarter and stronger than you're giving yourself credit for," she replied lazily. "If you'll excuse me, these trips always make sleepy." She leaned against the squabs and closed her eyes.

Well, drat, the first decent conversation she and the dowager countess had had since Savannah's arrival, and the countess feigned being tired. There were questions Savannah wanted to ask. She watched the older woman for a moment before opening the book she'd brought along.

She didn't get far in her reading, because the next thing Savannah remembered was waking up as the carriage flew over a hole in the middle of the road.

GABRIEL SAT at the large mahogany desk in his London home, Clevedon House, reading a stack of papers sent by his solicitors regarding the holdings of the late Lord Dawson. He'd been over them in part once before, but that was more about the estate and holdings of the earldom itself. He needed to know what shape it was in and where it needed to be turned around.

This report dealt with the late Roland Dawson's estate. What was left from an inheritance he received from his grandfather, how Dawson made his money. It seemed everything pointed back to the family plantation in the Caribbean. His ships took goods there, and he brought back spices, sugar, and other items that had a large market.

Then he saw something he never expected. Three of Dawson's ships had been lost at sea in one year, all after they'd picked up a shipment from the port near his plantation. One per month. While this had depleted Dawson's fleet by three, it hadn't kept him from purchasing three more from a yet unknown source. He ran his hands through his hair and sat back in his chair.

He knew the plantation, which was now young Vincent's, and as the young boy's personal assets was certainly his largest source of income. The small fleet should generate a good amount of revenue as well. Spices and other exotic things were still in great demand in England.

His mind kept returning to the lost ships. Certainly, a man could have a streak of bad luck, but it seemed Roland Dawson had endured more than his fair share. In the past year, a total of three ships had perished at sea. How had no one thought that odd? Even odder was the fact that one of the ships that had disappeared two years ago had been carrying Roland Dawson himself. His brother, Timothy, had continued the business his brother had set up. Nothing changed. Seven ships had been lost since Roland disappeared at sea. Gabriel needed to have his people dig into this further. What was more needed was for him to go to the docks and speak with some of the men at the warehouse owned by the late earl and the late Roland Dawson. Together, Gabriel found the brothers owned a few pieces of property together. A building here, a ship there, never enough to draw notice. Until now, and he would get to the bottom of it all.

Gabriel doubted that Savannah knew of these matters. Her father and brother had taken charge of her late husband's affairs as her brother was an American lawyer and kept a rather large practice outside Boston.

He rose and walked across the room to where he kept a selection of liquor decanters. He picked up the French brandy and poured a glass. As he swirled the dark amber liquid, he pulled out his timepiece.

Glancing down, he noted it was about time for him to prepare for this evening's event, the annual concert the Dowager Duchess of Hastings was holding. She had done so since before her late husband died, and it was still one of the premier events to be invited to. It wasn't huge and pretentious, but the duchess had a keen sense of whom to invite, including people like himself, who appreciated the musicians she hired from the Continent. Some years, there might be an operatic singer to enhance the music; others, it was simply the small ensemble she put together. Afterward, the duchess served light refreshments, and he usually used this as an excuse to leave. Not that he didn't enjoy the food served, it just gave him an opportunity to depart. The last thing he wanted was to feel as though he was being cornered by an adoring mother in search of a well-titled peer for her daughter.

Would Mrs. Dawson be in attendance this evening? The feelings he had about her whenever she was in a room were unsettling. Gabriel caught himself thinking about her, carnal, lustful thoughts he probably shouldn't be having. Not only was she the widow of a dear friend, love had turned out disastrously for him before. He found himself wanting to touch her, to run his tongue and lips across her smooth, silky skin. His base feelings went further. He wanted to taste her, to feel every part of her body. Her scent even made his cock harden, and he knew, despite his misgivings, he wanted to make her his.

CHAPTER 9

Savannah was admiring a group of potted orange trees that had been brought in from the duchess's conservatory. She had never seen one before. The closest she ever got was listening to Roland tell her about all the marvels to be found in the Caribbean. He enthralled her with stories of the lime, lemon, and orange trees that grew there.

"Granny has always had a fondness for oranges. Pineapples too," a young woman said from behind.

Savannah turned to find a woman close in stature to her, with flaming red hair and piercing green eyes. Immediately, she was entranced. She'd never seen a woman with such unique beauty.

"Lady Asher is your grandmother?" Savannah asked.

"Yes. I'm Fiona MacGregor. My mother is the youngest of Granny's children. Also the most rebellious. She married a Scot just because she knew her mother had a distaste for them." She smiled warmly.

"My mother-in-law is much the same way."

Fiona arched a brow. "How's that?"

"The dowager countess isn't fond of Americans, especially in her family, but I'm afraid she's stuck with us."

"Us?"

"Me and my son, Vincent, who's now the earl."

"We ought to get along famously," Fiona declared. She looked around the room. "It's time. Would you care to sit with me? It appears Lady Dawson is caught up in conversation with my granny and some of the other older women."

"Thank you. I dread things like this since I don't know anyone."

Savannah followed Fiona to a row of chairs in the center of the room. They were divided into two sections. People were beginning to take their seats as well, and fortunately, Fiona was able to find two nearest the outside. Savannah hated feeling trapped and was grateful her newfound friend didn't lead her inside.

The music was just starting when a tall, imposing figure sat down two rows in front of them. It took Savannah a moment to realize the well-dressed man was the duke. From her angle, the only thing she could tell was he wore a well-tailored black jacket. A young woman wearing a dark-rose gown moved three seats over in order to sit next to him. She wished she was closer so she could hear their conversation, because the duke didn't appear very happy with this intruder.

"She certainly has some nerve, assuming the duke would want a companion," Fiona quipped.

"Who is she?"

"Miss Augusta Statton. Her father is Viscount Hastings. The chit practically throws herself at Clevedon every time she runs into him. She's determined he's going to marry her."

Savannah shook her head. "I very much doubt the duke can be made to do something he doesn't want to do. He strikes me as that sort of man."

"I didn't realize you knew him."

"He's a neighbor of ours, and he's also taken on the

responsibility of seeing to my son's upbringing, with some persuasion from Lady Dorset."

"Beware of Miss Statton, then. She won't be pleased when she learns this."

"I don't see how it should concern her one way or another."

The music started. Chopin. Not one of her favorite composers, but to hear his music played by some of the finest musicians was cause for her to take notice of the complexity of his compositions.

Savannah caught herself staring in the duke's direction, Miss Statton seated next to him with a subtly smug smile. She couldn't imagine the duke being remotely interested in her. She wasn't particularly beautiful, just ordinary, with mousy-brown hair swept up off her neck.

They reached the end of the program, and Miss Statton could only allow Gabriel to leave to speak with other guests. Savannah noted her eyes never left his retreating figure as he bowed and proceeded back down the aisle. Would he see and acknowledge her, or would he pretend not to recognize her?

To her great surprise, Gabriel stopped in front of her. Beneath his jacket, he sported an elegant sapphire waistcoat with a crisp white shirt. His cravat matched the waistcoat in color. He was most definitely his own man.

"Miss MacGregor, Mrs. Dawson. How nice to see you both this evening. I thought it was one of the best performances of Chopin I've heard in a number of years."

Savannah glanced directly at him and smiled broadly. She caught a glimpse of Miss Statton standing with a group of young women, her gaze never leaving the duke as she scowled in his direction.

"I have to agree with you, Your Grace," Fiona replied.

"It was lovely," was all Savannah could manage. What was it about this man that made her all tongue-tied? What concerned her most was that she was unable to get a reading of what he might be thinking. This had never happened to her before.

"Are you in Town for long?" Fiona inquired.

"A fortnight at the most. I have a great deal of business to accomplish while I'm here. I'll be quite ready to return to the country by the time I'm finished."

Savannah was just about to comment when she noted Fiona's face change. She was attempting to subtly let her know they had unwelcome company. Miss Statton promptly inserted herself into the conversation. It was an awkward situation because Savannah had never had to deal with such obvious rudeness.

"Your Grace, I trust you'll stay for refreshments?" Miss Statton trilled.

"I'm afraid I won't. Not this evening."

Miss Statton, however, pressed on in a futile attempt to change his mind. Savannah caught herself smiling in Gabriel's direction as he firmly rebuffed her insistence he remain.

"You really should stay and partake, Your Grace. It's been so long since any of us has seen you."

"I appreciate the kind offer, Miss Statton, but I must decline."

He ignored the second part of her comment, knowing she was attempting to bait him. Savannah caught him looking in her direction. As usual, his expression was hard to read. The only way Savannah knew he wasn't to be persuaded was by the tone of his voice. He took his leave, and the last Savannah saw of him was his back as he walked toward the front door.

Miss Statton, of course, had no interest in carrying

on a conversation with either her or Lady Fiona, which was probably not a good thing on her part. She was in part snubbing her hostess by her rude behavior.

"Is she always like that?" Savannah asked her new friend.

"She is whenever the duke is near."

"I'm surprised she gets invited to anything."

"Granny only invites her because my mother and hers are friends."

"So she tolerates Miss Statton," Savannah said.

"Barely. One thing you'll learn about Miss Statton is that she's quite spoiled. She has four brothers and is the only girl. Her father dotes on her."

Savannah gazed across the room and saw her mother-in-law trying to get her attention. Lady Dorset had mentioned she wanted to leave early as they had an appointment with her modiste the next day. "I must apologize. The countess is ready to leave."

"That's perfectly all right. We really need to get together for tea, you know."

"Yes, we do."

"Tomorrow, perhaps?"

"I'm afraid the dowager countess is dragging me off to her modiste for a new wardrobe. I believe she thinks we Americans dress like savages."

Fiona laughed lightly. "Granny thought the same thing, that Scots are barbarians."

"And are Scots barbarians?"

"Hardly, and Granny has long since forgotten she at one time thought like that."

"That's because she has a beautiful granddaughter."

Fiona glanced over at the two women. "You'd best go. The dowager countess is looking as though she's going to spit if you don't."

～

GABRIEL HAD SEEN her the moment he walked into the room. There was no mistaking her, even from behind. Her golden tresses were swept up off her long, elegant neck. He caught himself wondering what it would be like to kiss his way down such a neck. If she was nervous about being here, she hid it well. He was aware it was her first social event in London, and, knowing the dowager countess, it would be far from her last.

He noted she was sitting with the dowager duchess's granddaughter, Lady Fiona. It didn't surprise him at all the two of them would find each other. Both were outsiders, not proper English women, Lady Fiona having been raised in Scotland and, of course, Savannah being born and bred in America. Quite different settings, but at the same time, similar.

He walked past them just as the music was about to start and sat a couple of rows in front of them. Savannah having interrupted his thoughts made him forget to look and see with whom he'd be sharing seating.

Before he knew it, Miss Statton had slid down several chairs and sat next to him. She was not the sort of woman he'd ever involve himself with. He'd tried subtly over the three years since she'd come out to convey that he wasn't interest, but even that didn't deter her from trying. Her brother Thomas said it well: when Miss Statton set her sights on something, no matter what, she didn't give up until she had what she wanted. All he could do was hope someone else would catch her fancy.

The night was still young, and rather than go home, Gabriel decided to stop by White's for a drink and masculine conversation. He'd learned through the years that men gossiped just as badly as women, and if you were seeking information on someone, sometimes going to a club was the best way to learn things.

As soon as he walked through the doors, he spotted Parr, his old friend. Parr beckoned him to join him.

"I didn't expect to find you here so late. Not just having arrived in town."

"I was in need of good drink and a dinner," Gabriel replied.

"Didn't want to dine alone at home?"

Gabriel smiled. "Something like that."

He motioned to a footman and ordered a brandy and dinner. "Join me?" he asked his friend.

Parr nodded. "I believe I will," he replied. He took a sip of his drink. "What really brings you here this late?"

"No reason. I was at a concert earlier and thought I'd drop by. Too early to go home. If I did, I'd only lock myself away in my study and work."

"You work too hard, Clevedon. You need a diversion of some sort."

Gabriel shook his head, smiling. "Perhaps I will once I get the young earl's estate in order. I've found it's more complicated than I anticipated."

"What do you mean?"

"Having been overseen by the family solicitor and the dowager countess, the estate's books are quite untidy."

"That's why she asked your assistance, isn't it?"

"That and the fact the boy's never learned anything about being a gentleman, let alone an earl. He's young, which makes it easy. The estate's revenues haven't been seriously looked at in years, and it shows."

"I thought you hired your solicitors to do the work?"

The footman returned with their drinks and informed them dinner would be ready shortly.

Gabriel took a drink of brandy. "I have. They're doing a more thorough audit. I'm meeting with them tomorrow."

"Think you'll find anything out of the ordinary?"

"I already have. Ships went missing. Too many of them. I'm also looking at Mrs. Dawson's estate as well, and that is where it gets interesting."

"How do you mean?"

"I'm afraid it's too early to tell, but there are some things that disturb me about how her husband ran his businesses. I can't say more until I'm certain."

"I'm sure if anyone can sort it all out, it's you," Parr replied with a grin.

The footman approached, and both men rose from their chairs. Gabriel then realized just how hungry he really was.

He also was amazed at how lovely Mrs. Dawson had looked. Looking into her estate meant spending more time with her, and he certainly was anticipating that. She stirred feelings in him that had been dormant far too long.

CHAPTER 10

It was a beautiful sunny day when Gabriel mounted his stallion. Too good a day to waste sitting inside a carriage. His first stop was to his solicitors to see if they'd finished their audit of the earl's ledgers and estate. Since Vincent's late father's business and money would eventually become his, Gabriel had also taken it upon himself to have Roland Dawson's affairs audited. He'd made notes of what he found odd or inconsistent and now had even more things he wanted them to delve deeper into.

The biggest thing he found odd with Roland Dawson's business was the number of ships lost at sea. Far more than usual for any shipping firm. Either Mr. Dawson hired incompetent men to run his ships or he had extremely bad luck. Remembering Roland, he failed to see where either could be the answer. Roland had been an astute businessman, one who'd helped his brother, the late earl, increase the income of the earldom.

He brought his horse to a stop in front of the offices of Smythe and Smythe and dismounted. He tied the stallion and walked indoors. He was shown into the office of Daniel Smythe, who had been handling the dukedom's affairs since his father's death. As part of an old family firm, Daniel had inherited the Duke of Clevedon's business when his father died. It was the only thing the duke and Daniel Smythe really had in common, though Smythe had an uncanny sense for finding wrongdoings.

"Good morning, Your Grace. Tea?" Smythe inquired as he showed Gabriel into his office. The room was filled with books and papers. He wondered how Smythe could even know where anything was in such disarray.

"Thank you, no," he replied, sitting in a well-worn leather chair on the opposite side of the large oak desk.

Smythe sat and was silent for a moment, as though he were choosing his words carefully. Finally, he sat forward in his chair. "The earldom is in good shape, in spite of the dowager countess's spending."

"Doesn't she receive an allowance?"

"Yes, but there were some expenses that exceeded her quarterly funds and were actually not covered by her allowance."

Gabriel sat up, his interest piqued. "I would assume she came to you to have the funds approved first?"

Smythe shook his head. "She did not, and by the time I received the bills, it was too late to stop."

"What exactly did she need extra monies for?"

"To redo her suite of rooms in both London and at Sky View."

"I believe I know how to remedy this situation. Write her dand tell her in the future all purchases or work must be approved in writing by your office. You and I can discuss it from there, though I think the countess will be more frugal."

"Agreed, Your Grace."

"The earldom's expenses should drop quite a bit until Vincent gets older. I'll make a point of meeting with the estate manager once a month, and if everything seems to be in order, I'll move it to once a quarter."

"That will work, Your Grace, as long as Lady Dorset understands."

"She will," he replied. "Anything else with the Earl of Dorset's matters?"

Smythe picked up a sheaf of papers. "I think you'll find it all outlined here, Your Grace."

"Excellent."

"Moving on to Mrs. Dawson and her husband's estate. I'm still working on it. Long distance makes it harder to get information in a timely manner."

"Do you need to go to America?"

"No, Your Grace. I have a good relationship with the late Lord Dorset's solicitors, and they're being most helpful."

"I'm sure they are. What have you found out?"

Smythe tapped the desk with his fingers. "I'm not sure what to make of it yet, Your Grace, but Lord Dorset liquidated a substantial portion of his holdings just before he died."

"Liquidated? What did he do with the funds?"

"That's what I'm still looking into."

This was something Gabriel hadn't anticipated. He studied a landscape on the solicitor's wall for a minute. "How bad is it?"

"Mrs. Dawson's husband left substantial debt."

"After two years, nothing has been done about it?"

"No, his solicitors have been working on the matter, but I'm afraid by the time all is paid, the widow will have little left."

Gabriel ran his fingers through his hair. This wasn't

what he thought he'd hear. How could a man leave his family like this, and what had he done with the funds he'd received? There were too many unanswered questions at this point, much to Gabriel's dismay. "Is there enough to give her a decent allowance?"

"She could be afforded something, but at this point, until the matter is closed, I would suggest against it."

"Then set it up so she gets funds from the earldom. She is his mother. The amount can be decreased once her late husband's estate is in order."

"As you wish, Your Grace."

"I'm quite interested in what Dawson did with all that money. Did his people have any idea?"

"None, Your Grace. I'm working on it, along with his people in America."

"Keep me apprised. Have someone look more closely into his shipping firm. Something isn't right."

"He did have substantial losses, losing so many ships in such a short amount of time."

"Agreed, oh, and look into the family plantation in the Caribbean. It's technically the earl's now, and I know his father made a great number of trips there. See if there's anything amiss."

"I've already been in contact with the plantation's estate manager. I requested copies of the ledgers and any other pertinent information."

Gabriel arched a sardonic brow. "His response?"

"He will put it all together and have it sent to me, Your Grace."

"Good, good. Let me know when it arrives and you've had a chance to read it."

"I shall."

"Is there anything else?" he asked as he rose from his chair. He'd spent enough time here poring over estates and money.

"No, Your Grace. I believe that's everything for now."

Gabriel shook hands with Smythe. "I'll be in town for a fortnight should anything further develop."

The man nodded, and Gabriel walked out of the office, a sheaf of papers in a leather pouch under his arm. He was both pleased and disturbed by what he'd learned today. Now, should he inform Mrs. Dawson of his findings, or let it wait until he had more information? He decided to wait unless she pressed him.

~

"This came for you, madam," Oswald said as Savannah and the countess entered. He was quite tall and, like Higgins at Dorsett Manor, had been in service since a young age.

"Thank you," Savannah replied as she lifted the sealed paper from the silver tray in Oswald's hands.

She handed the package she carried to Norma, who'd come out of nowhere, something Savannah still wasn't used to.

She and Lady Dorset had spent hours at her modiste's, studying fashion plates, choosing fabrics, and procuring Savannah an entire new wardrobe. New ball gowns, day dresses, riding attire, and undergarments had all been ordered. Savannah was impressed the woman even had a small selection of dresses and undergarments for sale in her shop, and figured the woman must employ a small army of seamstresses to fill orders, as her shop was full of women waiting for their turn with the French-born-and-trained woman.

"Who is it from?" Lady Dorset inquired.

Savannah turned it over. She recognized the ducal seal. Slowly, she broke the seal and opened the missive. "It's from the Duke of Clevedon."

She quickly scanned the contents, knowing the countess would be pressing her in a moment for its contents.

"What does His Grace want?"

"He wishes to meet with me to discuss an urgent matter."

Savannah didn't mention the time because she knew the countess would still be abed. The woman rarely rose before noon unless she had a pressing engagement. Rising late was another thing Savannah couldn't get used to.

"Does he say what's so urgent?"

She shook her head. "No."

"Don't forget we have the Duke and Duchess of Liverpool's ball to attend tomorrow evening." Lady Dorset arched a brow as she passed Savannah to head upstairs. "It might do you good to lie down, my dear."

"Yes, my lady. I will after I write the duke a reply."

She was staying in this evening, but knew Lady Dorset had plans with some of her friends. She was glad not to have to dress and go out. It would give her some time alone, perhaps to read.

Her thoughts drifted back to the duke and what his missive might mean. What could be so important? She knew he was to meet with his solicitors about the earldom, and that he was also going to have them dig into Roland's estate. Roland had been one of those men who thought women weren't able to think for themselves and only let her know what he wanted her to hear.

She climbed the stairs and walked down the hall to her rooms. She heard Norma busy in the dressing room with her purchases. At least her maid should be happy she was purchasing a more fashionable wardrobe. She'd never needed an elaborate wardrobe in America, but here, she was the mother of an earl, and in England, that was important.

Sitting at the small writing desk that sat against the pale yellow wall, Savannah found a sheet of paper and began to pen a reply to Gabriel. She told him she looked forward to seeing him the next day. The countess always seemed to be around whenever the duke paid a visit, which made her wonder why, and whether Lady Dorset would insert herself into Savannah's time with the duke.

Finishing her missive, she called to Norma, who came running from the dressing room.

"I need you to see this is delivered immediately to the Duke of Clevedon."

"Yes, madam." The young woman lingered for a moment, as though unsure if she should do as Savannah asked.

"Is there a problem, Norma?"

"No, madam. Yes, madam. The countess, she wants to see all your correspondence before it's delivered."

Savannah checked her temper. How dare Lady Dorset. She had no business reading or interfering with her correspondence. "I'll take care of Lady Dorset. Unless you wish to lose your position, please do as I ask and see this is delivered immediately to His Grace. Do I make myself clear?"

The maid bobbed, took the folded and sealed note, and fled. How dare Lady Dorset undermine her and her maid. If Savannah weren't so furious, she would confront the countess this very minute. Instead, she decided it best to wait until she calmed down.

Sitting on the side of the bed, Savannah removed her boots to lie down for a while. She was more worn out than she originally thought, more now that she found out the countess was intercepting her mail. She couldn't wait to see what sort of excuse Lady Dorset might have when confronted with the facts. The older woman was far wilier than Savannah had first given her credit for. If she didn't put a stop to it now, her mother-in-law would never stop. She likely expected that with Savannah being new to England and the ways of the peerage, she wouldn't question what she did. Little did she know that Savannah was going to respond in a way she couldn't imagine.

CHAPTER 11

$\mathcal{P}$romptly at two o'clock the next afternoon, the Duke of Clevedon arrived. Ever since Savannah received his missive, her curiosity had grown. There was something important he wanted to discuss with her. He had mentioned going to visit his solicitors on Vincent's behalf, to whom he'd sent the estate ledgers and other paperwork.

She dressed in a new dark-rose-colored muslin dress and had fussed more than usual while getting ready for the duke's arrival.

He strode into the drawing room with airs, wearing a well-tailored dark gray suit with a white shirt and light gray cravat. His golden-brown hair hung around his collar in waves, the sun picking up shades of red highlights.

"Good afternoon, Your Grace," she said. She had been standing by the hearth when he arrived.

"Mrs. Dawson." He took her hand in his and bowed over it. She felt a tremble go through her limbs at the touch of his hand. His tempting, masculine scent of leather and fresh air wafted to her.

"Tea, Your Grace?"

"Please. While we're waiting, would you care to take a turn in the garden?"

She thought it an unusual request, one normally reserved for couples who were courting or who had an interest in each other. Curiosity got the best of her. "Of course," she replied.

He led her outside to a gravel path. They walked slowly in silence for a few minutes until he stopped and gazed down at her. "I apologize for being so mysterious. I thought we'd have more privacy if we spoke out here."

"We could have spoken in the drawing room. The countess hasn't been down yet today."

"Part of what I need to say concerns her, which in turn will affect you."

He went on to tell her about the countess's spending habits and how he was going to put a halt to it.

Savannah bit her lip. "You're right, she's not going to like it."

"No, and I'll have the discussion with her. Since Timothy died, she seems to believe she can spend the earldom's money as she wishes."

"She receives an allowance, doesn't she? Perhaps it should be increased."

He nodded and began to walk again. "Already done. I'm also setting you up as well. You are the mother of the earl and should have money at hand for fripperies."

"Thank you, Your Grace."

"No need to thank me. I'm concerned your husband's estate may be consumed by his debt. The losses of his ships depleted his fortune. Of course, now that Vincent is the earl, you should not be concerned. It is a mystery, however, what happened to the loans and investments your husband received."

"I thought his solicitors did audit the estate," she replied.

"They had, but there are some discrepancies I think should be looked into."

Curious, Savannah lifted a brow. "Very well. I can't imagine what it could be. Roland was home so rarely, and when he was, he never spoke to me about his business affairs. I trust you know what's best, and that you'll keep me informed when the solicitors have finished."

"You'll be the first to know."

She smiled. She knew he had her and Vincent's best interests at heart. Though she knew how to keep books, managing something as complex as Roland's shipping business and other interests was best left to someone like Clevedon.

She herself was drawn to him, something she wasn't sure how she felt about. He was attentive and listened to whatever she had to say. He didn't seem to regard her as some mindless female who couldn't hold a conversation with a man unless it was about the weather or perhaps a rose. One could only say so much about the weather. Oh yes, and he was terribly handsome. So much so, Savannah thought there should be some sort of law regarding men's beauty.

"Thank you, Your Grace. For everything you're doing for Vincent and me."

"You're welcome," he said. "Your name, Savannah... It's very unusual."

"Very American," she replied with a smile.

"Yes, I suppose so. Isn't there a town by that name?"

"There is. It was where my parents met."

"Fascinating. I've never been to America. Never had a reason."

"Perhaps someday you will," she said. She glanced toward the house. "Shall we go in?"

"Yes."

They walked back to the house, where Gabriel followed her into the drawing room. "I'll ring for tea," she said quietly.

She sat across from him as they waited. They spoke about their literary preferences as they waited.

A moment later, a knock on the door came, and the butler and footman entered with a silver tray holding a pot of tea and two cups.

She handed Gabriel a cup and took her own. She caught him gazing at her over his teacup. Surprisingly she was at ease with this. She wanted to know what he was thinking, if he was attracted to her as she was to him.

"What are your plans while in Town? Besides going to the modiste?" he finally asked.

"I'm not sure. I know there is a ball in a couple of days, and I'm sure there will be more invitations. The dowager countess is taking care of all that."

"Perhaps you'd like to accompany me to the theater one evening. From what I understand, there is a very well put together production of Shakespeare. *A Midsummer Night's Dream*, if I'm not mistaken," he said before taking a sip of tea.

"I've never seen Shakespeare performed before. Not professionally, that is."

"Then we must go."

"I would like that very much, Gabriel." She couldn't believe it. What was happening here? Her heart was beating faster. Was it because she was simply sitting next to him? Was it lust? Her body was acting in ways it hadn't in years.

He leaned down. My God, he was going to kiss her!

And kiss her he did! He kissed her deeply, and as he did, desire coursed through her body.

· · ·

HER MOUTH WAS hot as he thrust his tongue inside. She moaned at the sensation. She grasped his shoulders as he pulled her closer. She tasted of salt and honey. Then he realized where they were and abruptly ended the kiss. He wanted more. Dear God, he wanted her more than he'd wanted any woman in years…since… No, he wouldn't ruin this moment.

"I believe I could use another cup of tea," he said. "I apologize for losing control."

Lust still coursed through his veins, and he knew as he'd known during that kiss that she was meant to be his. In his eyes, she was the most beautiful woman to walk the earth. She possessed an air about her none of her English counterparts could match. She wasn't shy, and she didn't giggle. Instead, she carried herself like a queen. She smoothed her skirts.

He tried to steer the conversation to safer topics than kissing. "The Duke and Duchess of Liverpool's ball is this evening. I trust you and Lady Dorset will be attending." Knowing the dowager countess, she wouldn't miss being seen at one of the premier summer events. Any time the duke and duchess had a social event, people waited anxiously for their invitation.

"Yes, we'll be there. And you?"

"Yes, I'll be there. At least for a while."

"You don't care for social events, do you?"

He nodded. "Not particularly, though I tolerate them because it's what's expected."

"Then that's a good quality, being a duke and all. You can pick and choose what events you attend."

"Quite true. I can."

He watched her as she daintily sipped her tea. She seemed to be deep in thought and avoiding his gaze. This was probably the first time since Roland had died that she'd been kissed, and he was glad it had been him.

Her fingers softly touched her lips before she appeared to remember they were in the middle of a conversation. "You will inform me of your solicitor's findings regarding Roland's estate?"

"Yes, of course."

"Was it because of Vincent you decided to audit Roland's estate?"

"Partially. I had some questions while I was going over the paperwork myself and thought they could best answer them if they simply audited everything."

She pushed a few stray hairs behind her ear and put her cup on the table in front of her. "I'm grateful to have someone like you looking out for Vincent and me."

"Roland was a dear friend, and I'm sure he'd do the same for me if our roles were reversed."

"He would."

Gabriel wondered how she was going to react when she found out her beloved husband wasn't the stand-up gentleman he had appeared to be. Most of Gabriel's inquiries wouldn't alert anyone. He was doing a routine audit on behalf of the Earl of Dorset, which extended to monies and property left by his father. This included the plantation obtained by Roland. The very one his friend had kept making business voyages to.

"Your Grace?" He heard Savannah's lilting voice in the background of his thoughts.

"I apologize. Wool-gathering, I suppose. You were saying?"

"I was asking if you knew if any of Roland's ships were in London."

He shook his head. "I'm afraid I don't. Easy enough to find out. Why?"

"I should like to see one. Also his warehouse."

"The docks are no place for a lady," he replied.

"Yes, I know, but I'd like to see what it is my son now owns. Besides," she said with a confident smile, "I always carry a pocket pistol Roland gave me and taught me to use."

"That's hardly sufficient." But Gabriel let out a long sigh. He knew she wouldn't give the matter up until she had her way. One thing he'd learned about her was that Savannah was very persistent.

"Let me check and see if one's in port first," he replied. "I'll take you one time and one time only. As I told you, the docks are no place for a lady, regardless of how strong she may be."

She shook her head, her pink tongue darting out of her mouth, licking her lips and getting Gabriel's attention immediately. "What could possibly happen in the middle of the day? Surely no one would accost me."

"You'd be surprised. A well-to-do lady such as yourself portrays money to them. You would be considered easy prey."

"I suppose you want me to reconsider."

"I would advise it, yes."

She smiled. "Just like you kissed me?"

"Kissed you? You kissed me, madam," he replied, amused by how she quickly changed subject matter.

She gave a breathy laugh and patted her hair. "I can assure you it was you who kissed me."

"That's not how I remember it," he replied.

"Then you have a very short memory, Your Grace."

For a second, he wasn't sure whether she was teasing him. And how had she jumped from wanting to visit the docks to the kiss they shared earlier?

He rose from his chair. He needed to get out of here, away from her. She was too intoxicating, and he was afraid he was no match for her. "Thank you for the tea. I shall see you tonight at the ball."

"I look forward to it, Gabriel," she replied. Hearing her name spoken in her American accent made him want to kiss her senseless, but the dowager countess was most likely lurking around some corner. She was the last person he wanted to run into right now. This evening would be another matter entirely. A more enjoyable time, and the countess would more than likely busy herself with her friends.

He strode out of the drawing room and out to his stallion, who had been brought around from the mews behind the house. As he rode away, Gabriel realized he was in danger of losing his heart to the American widow, something he'd vowed never to do again.

CHAPTER 12

Savannah was hard-pressed not to stare as she entered the ballroom at Lady Dorset's side. Above, four chandeliers hung from the ceiling, their crystals sparkling like miniature stars. Along one wall, mirrors were draped with garlands of flowers and gold and silver silk. Another large arrangement hid the musicians from view.

"How splendid! I've never seen anything so beautiful," Savannah exclaimed.

"Don't gawk, my dear. It isn't becoming," Lady Dorset muttered.

Savannah glanced around as they entered the ballroom. Heads turned toward them; people were staring and whispering. But why? Was it because she was American?

She looked up to see a rather tall gentleman with his wife beside him. She was petite and uncharacteristically thin. She wore a calm but slightly amused expression on her face.

"Mrs. Dawson. It's a pleasure to see you, as always," the gentleman drawled.

"Parr," the dowager countess replied dryly. "Lady Wexford. May I introduce Mrs. Savannah Dawson. As

I'm sure you've heard, she is my son Roland's widow. My dear, may I present the Earl and Countess of Wexford. Wexford and Roland attended Eton together."

"Always a pleasure to meet friends of my late husband," Savannah replied.

Lady Wexford smiled. "How are you liking London?"

"I enjoy what I've seen, though I can see why everyone leaves during the summer."

Beside her, Lady Dorset winced. Though it was perfectly acceptable for her mother-in-law to be to the point, she didn't approve when Savannah was blunt. Lady Dorset smiled stiffly.

"If you'll excuse us, I should like to introduce Mrs. Dawson to some of the other ladies."

Lady Dorset meant widows, matrons, and young ladies who'd never made a match. The group society now placed Savannah into whether she liked it or not. Another one of the things that bothered her about how women were treated.

Lady Dorset swept her across the room to a group and made introductions. Much to Savannah's disbelief, the dowager countess then turned and abandoned her, making some excuse about wanting to speak with their hostess.

Savannah politely spoke with a young woman next to her. The girl had never been married, and her parents promised one more season to find a suitable match, which meant whatever man would take her as a wife. The more seasons a woman had, the bleaker her choices became.

Glancing across the room, Savannah caught the dashing figure of the duke. Gabriel. He was politely speaking with two young women, whose mothers hovered in the background hoping for some sign of recognition for their daughters from Clevedon. Would he sign their dance cards? Savannah knew from her first encounter at a social event similar to this that the duke was not fond of dancing. Nor of being paired with any particular lady.

Suddenly, he glanced up, and their eyes met from opposite sides of the room. He nodded ever so slightly in her direction. She smiled and unfurled her fan. While she was grateful for his attention, she didn't want him to feel obligated to entertain her. His agreement with the countess had been made on Vincent's behalf. Anything else was of his own doing.

She imagined the duke had quite a long line of young ladies all vying for his attention. All they wanted was one glimmer of hope, no matter how small, that he might be interested. Though he'd failed to mention it to her, Savannah learned Clevedon had voiced an interest in taking a wife recently. He should, as a man of his position needed a wife to give him an heir. The future of his dukedom depended on it, though she didn't doubt Gabriel would have no problem finding a wife. She would be devastated of course. The thought of him with another woman, especially since that kiss, sent a wave of jealousy coursing through her. If there was any chance for them to have a relationship she didn't want to lose it.

She turned her attention back to the young woman, Miss Jane Collins. Her father, Savannah learned, was a viscount and quite the landowner in the northeast part of England. She had a likeable personality. Miss Collins was one of the few young women who didn't view Savannah being American as though she had the plague.

Gabriel was making his way across the ballroom toward her. Every female eye lingered on him as he ended the conversation he was having and smiled politely at the young woman. The orchestra was playing a rather lively number, so he had to walk along the edges of the ballroom, acknowledging everyone he passed.

"He's coming this way," Miss Collins observed.

"Who? Who's coming?" Savannah asked, as she feigned not knowing what Miss Collins was referring to.

"His Grace. He's headed this way as though he knows you quite well."

Savannah smiled. "You picked up on that merely by the way he walks?"

"No, but it is a well-known fact that the duke is assisting in the upbringing of your son. Rumor has it that it is merely a matter of time before he asks you."

"Asks me what?" Savannah asked genuinely confused.

"To marry him, of course."

Shocked, Savannah laughed. Was everyone that naive? The duke was merely being polite to her because of Vincent. There were no intimate, romantic inclinations between them. They shared a kiss, nothing more. "The duke is merely being polite. He was an old friend of my late husband."

"Yet I dare say he's set his sights on you, even if he is unaware of it."

This was the silliest thing she'd ever heard. As she was a lowly commoner and he a powerful duke, there could never be more between them than that stolen kiss. Eventually, he would find someone among the ton and marry. She did, however, wonder how their relationship would continue once he found his duchess. Not that it was any of her business. A twinge of jealousy reared its ugly head, but as he drew closer, that feeling changed to an emotion she hadn't experienced in years. Not since before Roland died.

~

GABRIEL LOOKED QUICKLY TWICE upon seeing Savannah. She stood across the room, speaking with Miss Collins, a young woman who'd been through several seasons without securing a match. Savannah was beautiful, probably the most beautiful woman in the room, dressed in a dark-gold confection that made her look like a goddess. It was daring, but daring was exactly what he expected from her. She wore pearl earbobs with a matching pearl choker and bracelet. She didn't belong with the matrons. She needed to be seen by all. However, to be seen by all meant other men would ogle her, and since their kiss, he now considered her his. Not for anyone's delight except his own.

Before he was halfway to Savannah, he felt an arm on his sleeve. He turned to see who the offending party was, for he knew by the touch it was not a female guest. His friend Henry Littleton, the Duke of Dover, stood there, a strange look on his face. Was it concern, or pity perhaps? He couldn't be sure. "Dover? You look as if something ails you."

"I need to speak with you in private."

Gabriel stared at his friend in disbelief. He was truly in some sort of anguish. "Now?" he asked, hoping Dover would decide the matter wasn't as urgent as he was making it out to be.

"Yes. It's a highly sensitive matter, and you need to hear it from me."

"What did you do this time, Henry?" he joked.

"I'm serious, Gabriel," he replied. One thing about Dover, he never used Gabriel's given name unless it was important. "There's a private sitting room one floor up. No one should bother us there. Meet me in ten minutes."

Gabriel sighed. "This better be good."

"It could be life-altering."

He shook his head. "Very well, ten minutes."

The two men parted. Gabriel was more than perturbed by his friend's insistence. As far as he was concerned, anything could wait until the following day. It had always irritated him that men had to use social gatherings as a means to conduct business. Nothing was that important.

As he neared Savannah and the other women, he greeted them as he always did. Evenings such as this were for entertainment. The ladies provided such entertainment simply by looking lovely. He took Miss Collins's hand and greeted her, then Mrs. Dawson. He was still completely enthralled by her beauty. She left him breathless.

"Mrs. Dawson, may I have the next waltz? I believe it's the dinner set."

"You may, Your Grace, if you'll sign my dance card. I would hate for another gentleman to insist it could be had simply because you forgot to sign it."

She handed him a pencil and the card. He signed the appropriate spot before returning it to her.

"If you ladies will excuse me, I need to speak with someone." He glanced at Savannah. "I'll be back momentarily. The Duke of Dover has requested a word."

"Your Grace," she replied.

He bowed to both ladies and continued through the ballroom. Taking the stairs two at a time, he quickly made it to the top, bypassing the card room the duke had set up. He walked down the hall until he came upon the closed door containing the family sitting room.

The small room was done in red damask wall coverings with matching chairs and settees. Henry paced in front of the fire.

"What is so damn important it couldn't wait until tomorrow?" Gabriel demanded.

"I know you're like a guardian for the young earl,

and that you're assisting Mrs. Dawson with her late husband's business affairs," he said. "What I have to tell you could be disturbing."

"Well? What is it?"

"There is a rumor going around that a man looking remarkably like Roland Dawson was seen at the docks yesterday."

Gabriel arched a brow. "You do realize he's dead."

"Yes."

"It must be someone who favors Roland, and whoever told you this is mistaken."

"I'm just telling you what I've heard. I'm not sure who else has heard it, but I thought you should know either way."

"I appreciate you sharing this with me."

"Didn't Mrs. Dawson have him declared legally dead?"

"Yes, after two years she petitioned the court in America and had him declared dead."

"Hmmm," Henry muttered.

"What? What is it?"

"I don't know. It seems odd a man of his standing would fake his own death. Makes no sense."

"Men have done more foolish things than that."

This wasn't at all what he wanted to hear, but what would he want? He needed to have men watch Sky View and their London home.

"Do you know which ship he came in on?" Gabriel asked.

"I was told he was seen boarding a ship to the islands," Henry replied. "Didn't Roland have a sugar plantation?"

"Yes, though it's being looked after by the estate manager."

"How are you going to handle this?"

Gabriel shook his head. "First of all, we don't even

know if it was Roland. One sighting of a person matching his description is reason to be on the lookout, nothing else."

"I'm merely relaying the information, Gabriel. What you do with it is up to you."

"And I appreciate you coming to me with it," he replied. He needed to speak with his solicitors and see what would happen should Roland indeed still be alive. The nagging thought was why would he pretend otherwise? Why on so many levels. First of all, Gabriel needed to verify what he'd just been told. He'd send a man down to the docks to ask around, see what ships had departed recently for the islands.

"What do you plan on doing, and don't tell me 'nothing,'" Henry said. "I can see your mind whirling about."

"I'm going to send a man to the docks to ask what ships have recently departed for the islands."

"I'll make some discreet inquiries around the docks myself. I know he owned a warehouse."

"Yes, he did. His widow wants to see it along with one of the ships her son now owns," Gabriel replied.

"Will you do it? Take her there?"

Gabriel arched a brow. "I'll put her off for as long as possible. However, Mrs. Dawson is not easily deterred."

Henry straightened his cravat. "I suppose we should rejoin the others."

Gabriel nodded before walking out of the small sitting room ahead of Littleton.

By the time he and Littleton rejoined the others in the ballroom, the next set had just begun. He found Savannah near the same spot where he'd last spoken with her. She smiled as their eyes met and he smoothed any worry from his expression.

"Mrs. Dawson, I believe this next dance is mine?"

She put her gloved hand on his arm and let him lead

her out to the middle of the ballroom. He caught her perfume; something light, like vanilla and oranges. It wasn't too heavy a scent, perfect for her. Something he would forever associate with her.

"I assume you and Littleton were able to have your conversation in peace. He seemed quite serious," she said as she put her hand on his shoulder.

"Littleton's always serious."

They began the waltz, saying nothing at first as couples whirled by. He could feel eyes on them, watching them. It was always like that for him, which was why he had such a distaste for social events. Although he didn't care and paid no mind to the gossip, somehow, with Savannah, it was different. It was as if he wanted nothing more than to take her back to the country and keep her to himself, away from prying eyes. But now there was the possibility her husband might still be alive. Why was he being so illusive? Would she go back to him, or was there a glimmer of hope for them?

She appeared to notice they were the focus of discussion as well. "It seems we are the center of attention. Everyone is watching us."

"Let them," he growled.

"I suppose I'm not too well liked by some of the mothers this evening. They feel as though I'm monopolizing your time."

"Ridiculous. I will dance with whomever I please and spend my time with whichever lady I want, and I choose you."

"I'm flattered, Your Grace. I must tell you, though, I'm not interested in marrying again. Not right now."

He laughed softly. "Neither am I, my lady, which is why I think we get along so well."

She blushed. "You're not interested in marriage, Your Grace?"

He hated when she called him by his title. He'd

much rather she address him by his given name. "Gabriel," he muttered. "I want to hear you say it." He drew her closer, his breath coming short as he realized that if Roland were still alive, he might never hold her in his arms again. "As for marriage? Perhaps, someday"

"But don't you need to be thinking about an heir? I believe I remember hearing somewhere that is quite important to you peers."

He rumbled, "It is, but I am a firm believer that when the time is right, it will happen."

"A proper English duchess will magically appear? Or will you find her amongst the ballrooms of London?"

The waltz was coming to an end. He didn't want it to end, ever. He found he was enjoying the warmth of her against his body far more than he probably should. Not for the first time, he cursed English society's rules.

"I'll know when I find my duchess."

Gabriel noticed Lady Dorset watching from the sidelines. She might be trying not to show her emotions, but he could read right through her. She was not happy he and Savannah were spending time together in such a public place. Knowing her, she was dreading the gossip and having to explain to those who didn't know just who Savannah was and what role he played.

He returned Savannah to Lady Dorset. They would be going in to supper, and as one of the senior peers, he would be among the first to be seated. It was how things were done.

The countess was accommodating as usual. How could she not be in front of all the other ladies? As well, he was sure by now she knew of the parameters he'd set regarding her allowance. She was the one who'd convinced him to go through the books and make sure everything was as it should be going forward for young Vincent.

"Lady Dorset, I have invited Mrs. Dawson to the theater to see a new version of *A Midsummer Night's Dream*. Would you care to join us?"

The dowager countess smiled crookedly. "Thank you for thinking of me, Your Grace, but I must decline. I'm sure Mrs. Dawson will be enthralled to see Shakespeare performed in his home country."

Gabriel nodded as the dinner bell sounded. "Ladies, if you'll excuse me."

"Thank you again, Your Grace," Savannah murmured.

"My pleasure."

The next few hours were going to pass too slowly as far as Gabriel was concerned. He had no interest in dinner conversation when he'd rather have a more stimulating one with Savannah. He tucked away what Dover had mentioned for future inquiries. That Roland could still be alive was unfathomable. Men did sometimes fake their own deaths, usually to escape financial ruin or, worse yet, to escape a crime committed.

The Roland he remembered would put his family before anything else. The Roland he knew had perished in a storm at sea two years ago. He couldn't afford to let himself think otherwise, because that would mean Savannah was still married. A thought he found himself unable to bear.

Gabriel led the others into dinner. His dinner companion for the evening was the Duke of Liverpool's daughter, Lady Compton, whose husband, the Earl of Compton, was abroad on the Continent. Gabriel could not have wished for a better dining companion, and silently thanked the Duchess of Liverpool for her astute choice. At least Lady Compton wouldn't sit and talk about the weather.

CHAPTER 13

*I*t had been with great reluctance Savannah left the ball, but when the countess was ready to leave, she knew she had no choice. The evening had been perfect, just as Lady Dorset had said it would be. Gabriel had been there. They'd danced twice, and even though she had been enthralled with him and his stimulating conversation, Savannah knew there would never be anything between them. There were far too many younger ladies wanting him to pay attention to them.

Then he angered her as quickly as he made her happy. She'd merely seen him at dinner as they were seated quite a'ways from each other. He caught her eye several times with a look of mirth in those green orbs. That was enough, until after dinner, when she found out he'd left abruptly without a word to her. Men did that, and could get away with such behavior. She, on the other hand, was forced to endure tea and gossip after dinner.

Today, he sent a message around stating he would call on her that afternoon. So now they were courting? Whatever it was, he wanted to take her for a carriage ride through the park. The day was beautiful, perfect for such an outing.

She finished writing a letter to Vincent, telling him all about what she'd seen so far and that she'd be home soon. Having never been apart from him, this separation ate at her like a dark hole. Writing him filled the void, at least temporarily.

She walked downstairs to find not a footman or even the butler to give her letter to. Sometimes she still couldn't keep straight what roles the various servants played. Some she thought overlapped, but she knew the English were quite set in their ways, and suggesting to the countess to change anything might be seen as meddling.

After finally finding the butler keeping vigil near the front door, she gave him her letter, then walked toward the drawing room. Fresh flowers filled a vase in the hall. Once in the drawing room, she saw two others, one slightly larger than the other two.

If the flowers were for her, why would anyone be sending her flowers? She failed to remember anyone except Gabriel who even remotely attracted her attention. To make matters stranger, there was no card for any of them.

Lady Dorset was seated on a chair, her needlework in one hand. She gazed up as Savannah entered the room.

"Good afternoon," Lady Dorset greeted her.

Savannah had moved to the largest bouquet of pink roses. There were at least two dozen blooms, and their fragrance enhanced the room. "These are magnificent."

"They are. You seem to have attracted the Duke of Clevedon's attention."

"They're all from him?"

"They are."

"He sent no card?" She studied the countess to see if

her facial expression changed. As usual, however, the woman's emotions were locked up tight.

"Yes, he did. They're over in my desk," she replied. "I didn't think the servants should see who they were from. It's highly inappropriate."

"What? What's inappropriate?"

"That the duke is sending you flowers and paying attention to you."

"He's overseeing Vincent's upbringing. Of course we're going to speak, but I wouldn't go as far as to call it paying attention to me. I can't stop him from sending me flowers either. That would be rude."

The countess arched a well-manicured brow. "Then you shouldn't lead him on."

Savannah stared at her in disbelief. "You think I'm leading him on? I can assure you, Lady Dorset, that's the furthest thing from my mind. The duke has merely become a friend and confidant." She realized she probably shouldn't have used the word confidant, but she blurted it out before thinking, and now it was out there.

"He's taking you to the park this afternoon. The theater as well? If that doesn't imply he's interested, I don't know what does." She sniffed.

"He's taking me to the park so I can see it for myself. There is nothing that old in America."

"Of course there isn't."

"Well, if you expect me to cancel our outing, you're going to be displeased, because I won't."

"No, I didn't expect you to."

Savannah stood there shaking. Not even her mother had ever spoken to her in such a manner. It wasn't as though she were a young debutante. She was a widow, and if a man wished to take her somewhere for an afternoon, he could. She turned back to the roses and smelled them once again.

"I thought we'd return to Sky View tomorrow," Lady Dorset announced. "I know you're missing young Vincent."

"Didn't you want to stay a fortnight or longer?"

The countess smiled sardonically. "I've finished what I came to do, and thanks to the Duke of Clevedon, I can't shop for a few items."

"What has the duke got to do with your shopping?"

"I made the mistake of putting him in charge of Vincent's affairs, which included the money. He's cut me off. I can't redecorate as I wanted. Not without getting permission for the extra funds that will be required."

It didn't sound like too much to ask. It wasn't her money, and from what Savannah had just learned, the duke was protecting her son's interests. "You could ask him for an increase in your allowance, couldn't you?"

"He already did, but it's hardly enough to cover the costs of what I need."

"Clevedon is a reasonable man. I'm sure if you approach him, he'll change his mind."

Shaking her head, the countess sighed. "No, he won't." She rose from her chair, putting her needlepoint down. "If you'll excuse me, my dear, I'm afraid I have a headache."

A headache wasn't what Savannah thought the countess was running from. She knew Gabriel was coming to take her out for a drive and didn't want to face another confrontation. Savannah smiled. Lady Dorset probably wasn't expecting her to stand her ground either. The countess was quite used to getting her way and had probably spent far more in the time since Timothy died than was necessary. Or that Gabriel thought she should be spending. She liked that about him. He watched out for her son. One of the many redeeming qualities she was beginning to like about the Duke of Clevedon.

~

THE FIRST THING Gabriel noticed as he handed Savannah into his phaeton was how quiet she was. For the life of him, he couldn't figure out what brought on this change. They had a nice enough time at the Duke and Duchess of Liverpool's ball. He'd paid as much attention to her as was socially appropriate, even if she was a widow. He detested gossip and wouldn't see her good name sullied by the old biddies wanting to keep Savannah's entrance into London society from becoming a success.

She remained quiet, even though he took the time to point out sights he thought might interest her. Rather than comment, she would simply nod. So uncharacteristic of her. Had he done something wrong?

They had just entered the park, and the line of carriages was thick. It seemed everyone was taking advantage of the beautiful weather. Having had enough of her silence, Gabriel carefully prodded her. "Are you all right? You seem awfully quiet this afternoon?"

She shook her head and focused on the greenery rather than look at him. "I'm fine, Your Grace. You mustn't worry yourself over nothing."

There it was, she was referring to him by his title. Something was indeed amiss. "May I be blunt?"

"Of course, Your Grace."

"Gabriel. Something has happened since the ball last night. Something is amiss, and I want to know what. Tell me. Please."

Carriages passed, people walked by his phaeton, all greeting him and looking on with keen interest. The

Duke of Clevedon never drove a carriage through the park. He always rode his black stallion.

They were nearing the serpentine. He saw a spot on the side open up and urged the pair of grays toward it.

He gazed at her thoughtfully. "Tell me, Savannah, what is wrong?"

"You really don't need to concern yourself. It's nothing."

"Please forgive me, but I don't believe you. Something has you upset, and I would like to know."

She sighed. "It's the dowager countess. She informed me we'd be leaving for Sky View tomorrow rather than a fortnight hence."

He cocked his head in thought. "That's rather sudden. Did she say why? Usually, she loves spending time in Town."

"I'm afraid it has to do with you. She's angry with you for cutting her funds and is going to punish me by cutting our time here."

Gabriel smiled. He'd hit a nerve with Lady Dorset, and she was going to do what she could to sabotage his interest in Savannah. "Did she mention I also gave her an increase in her allowance, and that she was the one who asked me to go over the earldom's finances?"

"Vaguely," Savannah replied. "She wants to redecorate and doesn't want to have to go through you or your man of business to do so."

He nodded. "I just bet she doesn't."

"So I'm afraid I won't be able to accompany you to the theater."

"Would you like me to speak with Lady Dorset, see if I can change her mind?"

"I would, but I'm afraid that would make matters worse for me. Besides, I miss Vincent something awful, so this is a way to see him sooner."

"Perhaps I could persuade her to let you remain in

London? I would accompany you back to the country as soon as my business is completed."

She nodded. "I would like that very much, Gabriel. Just don't push her too hard."

"I promise," he replied, his attention drawn to the pale-yellow dress she wore. He rarely noticed women's attire unless it was a ball grown, and they were usually magnificent. Savannah had an eye for fashion, but knew not to overdo the way so many of her contemporaries, including the countess, did.

"I just worry about Vincent. I don't need the dowager countess upsetting him by telling him some untruth."

Gabriel hadn't taken that into consideration. Lady Dorset was already taking his actions out on Savannah. She had a vindictive side and certainly didn't try to contain her dislike for the fact her daughter-in-law was American. Knowing how much Savannah adored her young son, he decided to make a counter proposal. "What if you returned with Lady Dorset? I'll return to Brook Fall as soon as my business is concluded. Perhaps in a few weeks, we could bring young Vincent to Town."

"He would love that," she replied. "You're sure you don't mind?"

"Not at all. I'm sure Vincent would love to see some of the sights."

"At his age?" she teased. "He is only seven."

Gabriel picked up the reins to move back into the long line of carriages. "I'm sure there's bound to be something he'd love."

The carriage pushed on, neither he nor Savannah saying much more. He acknowledged those he knew, but didn't stop because of the parade of people. All of a sudden, he heard Savannah gasp in disbelief. He turned to see she had one hand over her mouth, the other pointing forward.

"What is it?" he demanded. "What has upset you?"

She shook her head, unable to speak. For a moment, Gabriel believed she would surely faint on him. She just kept pointing.

"Savannah, what is it?" he gently prodded.

"Roland. I swear I just saw him heading toward that hill," she finally gasped.

Gabriel jerked his head in the direction she was pointing, but saw nothing but a wall of people out for a walk. This was the second supposed sighting of Roland Dawson. Could it be true that he hadn't drowned in a shipwreck? If it were indeed true, what did he want?

He took one of her hands in his. "I'm sure it was only someone who favored him. You know what they say, everyone has a twin somewhere in the world."

She nodded and looked up at him, shaken and pale. "Perhaps you're right. I hadn't thought of that, but he certainly looked like Roland."

"Come, I think you've had enough excitement. Would you like me to show you some of the sights?" He'd distract her for the afternoon, but clearly the need to discover the identity of Roland's impersonator was more urgent than ever.

CHAPTER 14

*T*hough she didn't like the circumstances under which her trip to London ended, Savannah had to admit she was glad to be back at Sky View. She found she missed the peace and tranquility of the country compared to the hustle and bustle of London.

Most importantly she'd missed Vincent. He was the most important person in her life. During the time since Roland had died, her son had provided her with happiness she might not otherwise feel. He made her realize she had a reason to strip herself of her mourning attire and live. Live for her son, and for herself. After all, time did have a way of healing all wounds.

The trip from London had been a strain, and Savannah chose to read a book she brought along rather than have to make polite conversation with the dowager countess. Fortunately, Lady Dorset napped most of the journey, making the time far easier.

The carriage came to a stop in front of the house. When all that appeared were the butler and two footmen, Savannah found herself disappointed. She'd halfway expected to see Vincent come bounding out the front door to greet her. Then she reminded herself that there probably hadn't been time to get word of their return, and if there had, the countess most likely made sure the information was withheld. After all, the older woman felt Savannah coddled the boy far too much and had made a point of reminding Savannah of that. In Savannah's mind, Vincent should get all her attention because in a few years, he would be going off to school and would have to fend for himself. Children were remarkably resilient, and she wished she could be as well.

Without a word, Savannah climbed the stairs. Rather than go to her room, she walked upstairs to the nursery. When she quietly opened the door, she discovered Vincent deep in arithmetic. She stood at the doorway and placed her fingers to her lips so the governess wouldn't stop.

"That's very good, Vincent," the governess said.

"Mama!" the young boy cried, then raced over to her waiting arms. Savannah knelt and hugged him back.

"Oh, how I missed you," she said, brushing a stray lock of hair from his face.

"I wasn't expecting you until next week. Wasn't London to your liking?"

"I was lovely. We just finished our appointments more quickly than we anticipated and decided to leave the heat of Town."

He nodded. "Did His Grace return home with you?"

"No, I'm afraid the duke had business to attend to. He promised to come see you the moment he returns."

"I'm glad, Mama. I missed you and the duke."

"Well, I'm back. Now you finish your lessons. I'm going to freshen up. Perhaps if you finish up your work, we can go for a walk or you can join me for tea."

"Oh, I'd love that! Tea is the best time. There are so many sweets to choose from, don't you think?"

"Yes, there are."

He did as he was instructed, and Savannah waited for a moment as her son recited numbers before disappearing to the sanctity of her own room.

Her maid was bustling about in the dressing room when she entered. Savannah stuck her head in and told Norma she wished to freshen up and change into a brown muslin dress. She was looking forward to seeing the duke again. She missed their talks when they were apart. He was becoming such an important part of her and Vincent's life, and she didn't care anymore who disapproved.

CHAPTER 15

Gabriel handed the reins of his stallion to a stable boy as he entered the courtyard, or what had once been known as a bailey. He was home and glad for it. He'd spent the past three days since Savannah had left combing the docks and other key places to see if he could indeed find this man who looked so much like Roland Dawson. Searching the docks was the logical solution once again since he had shipping interests.

"Make sure to cool him down and give him a good rub down," Gabriel told the young boy. "And see that he gets an extra ration of oats too."

"Yes, Your Grace," the stable boy replied as he led the massive beast away.

Was the man he sought indeed Roland, or just a man who happened to look a great deal like his late friend? Enough so that Savannah had been spooked by the sight of him?

Having not found the man or any trace of him, Gabriel assumed he had boarded a ship bound for who knows where. The possibilities were endless. He didn't have any more time to make inquiries. He had pressing matters here at home that needed his attention.

He went to his rooms and changed his dusty riding clothes for something clean. He was taking Savannah for an afternoon ride. Why he'd planned it for the day he returned, he wasn't sure, other than he was anxious to see her. He would take her back to the tower and then to the roof, where the view was spectacular. One could see for miles on a clear day.

He wrote her a short missive letting her know he'd arrived and would call on her in two hours. After applying the ducal seal to the missive, he handed it to his butler with strict instructions that the man delivering it was to make sure it was received by Mrs. Dawson. Simmons nodded and assured him it would be delivered directly to the young woman.

He walked into his study, shutting the door behind him. Staring at the pile of mail, invitations, and documents, Gabriel picked up a decanter of whiskey and poured himself a glass. He usually didn't partake this early in the day, but he was exhausted from the long ride. The demands of his position were never-ending. Always, something required his attention. He glanced at the mound of papers and ledgers. The majority could wait.

He called for the butler to make sure the tower had been cleaned. Knowing it hadn't been used for years, he didn't want Mrs. Dawson subjected to spider webs or vermin.

"Simmons, has the tower been cleaned as I asked before I left?"

"Yes, Your Grace. I believe you'll find it to your satisfaction."

"Good, good." He sat on the edge of his desk. "I think I'll walk out to the stables and see about having a suitable horse saddled for Mrs. Dawson."

"Yes, Your Grace. Is there anything else?"

"No, nothing right now."

Simmons left the study, closing the door behind him.

Gabriel waited until he was sure the butler had disappeared, something the man was good at when necessary. His staff knew when to appear and when not to, especially when there were guests at Brook Fall.

He walked out to the stables and chose a chestnut mare for Savannah. The mare was one of the thoroughbred-Irish Draught crosses he bred. She was well trained and not skittish, with a big heart. He motioned a stable boy to ready her for Savannah, and to have a youngster, a gray gelding, readied for him.

He rode at a quick pace, with the stable boy following to the Dawson estate.

Slowly after he arrived, he felt his heart in his throat as he caught a glimpse of Savannah. She wore a dark green riding outfit, which made her light blonde hair sparkle. Her deep blue eyes reminded him of two sapphires. He wanted nothing more than to kiss her, but now wasn't the time. Not only did he want their next kiss to be private, he didn't want to chance the dowager countess witnessing it, whether she hid in the shadows or not.

It had been a long time since he'd wanted to kiss a woman like he did Savannah. He'd thought he'd loved Marie, but what he felt when he held Savannah in his arms far surpassed any passion he'd known before.

"Good afternoon, Your Grace," Savannah said as she got closer. The lilt of her voice soothed him.

"Mrs. Dawson, you look radiant."

"Thank you."

"Are you ready? I picked out a mare specifically for you. I think you'll like her." Gabriel motioned for the stable boy to bring the mare around to the mounting block. She patted the mare on the neck before mounting. She gave him an odd look.

"What? Did I do something wrong?" he inquired.

"I don't require a side-saddle. I'm a good enough rider I can ride astride. These are dangerous, you know." She smiled.

He swung his leg over the back of the gelding. "I'll make sure my staff remembers that in the future. If you'd like I can have the mare resaddled. It would only take a few minutes."

"Thank you, Your Grace. I would appreciate that."

Not twenty minutes later, they rode quietly, side by side until they were out of sight of the house. Gabriel gathered his reins.

"I thought we'd ride out to the tower."

"Wonderful. Can we go up to the roof?"

He nodded. "Yes, it's been cleaned since our last visit."

She shortened the mare's reins and, in an instant, urged the horse into a gallop, leaving Gabriel in a cloud of dust. He galloped behind her, content to let her enjoy herself. She was an accomplished horsewoman, better than most women he knew. So many barely rode, preferring to be seen in a carriage. He couldn't recall ever riding like this with a woman besides his sister, Frannie. Henrietta had always been prim and proper, preferring painting and needlework to galloping across a field on horseback.

Finally, he caught up with her, and they slowed down. Coming upon a fork in the path, Gabriel led her down to the left. In a few more minutes, they'd be able to see the top of the tower. The tower had always been a fascinating place. The real reason for its construction was lost to history, given there were so many stories. One tale was it had been built to serve as a sort of prison of a home for a long-gone duke's mistress. Another was that the tower was built as a lookout for trespassers. The third was it was where his great-great-grandfather kept his wife, the duchess, who turned mad after a fever.

Gabriel liked to believe the second story. The idea of this structure being used for anything dark didn't sit well with him.

"You're being rather quiet," Savannah said, joining him as they slowed their horses to a walk.

"I was trying to recall the stories I was told about the tower growing up." He shared the three tales with her. She was amused as he went into detail.

"I think more than likely, the tower was built as a lookout. Unless, of course, you have well-founded evidence of one of the others."

"If there is, it's hidden in one of the books in the library. Dusty and forgotten."

She gazed ahead to where the top of the tower now appeared before them. "It would be nice to know, wouldn't it?"

"I suppose. I never gave it much thought."

"Has it just sat there empty?"

He nodded and stopped the gelding. "As far as I can remember, though I think my father did come here to be alone to think."

"I imagine the view would be a perfect deterrent from any troubles one might have."

He arched a brow. "You're about to find out."

She smiled back at him. "You're a strange man at times, Your Grace."

He sighed and shrugged. "I've been told worse."

Gabriel helped her down and found a tree to tie the horses. Opening the door, he followed her inside. Coming to the staircase leading to the roof, Gabriel continued to follow Savannah, watching the gentle sway of her hips as she took each stair. Something stirred within him, and he thought about the first time his father had brought him to the tower, how exciting it was to climb these exact same stairs for the very first time as a young boy. Now, all these years later, he was sharing the view with someone new.

"It's beautiful," Savannah exclaimed as they came through the door at the top of the stairs. She was right, the view was splendid, but he always loved to see the expression on another's face when they looked out and saw the land, which seemed to go on forever.

"It is, isn't it?" Gabriel replied, not knowing if he were asking her or simply making a statement.

She walked around to another side, the one facing south. The scenery was slightly different, lush green everywhere. The top of the castle was visible from this vantage point. "I can see why your ancestors built the tower here. You can see anyone approaching the castle."

He nodded, amazed by her grasp of the situation. Most woman wouldn't figure it out. "Yes, especially anyone approaching from London. You can see from all vantage points, but London would always have been where most came from, whether invited or not."

"It just sits unused now? Pity."

"I believe my parents and possibly grandparents used the tower. My mother and father used to take a meal up here in the summer, and my mother would sometimes come and read."

"I can see her attraction to the place. Has anyone ever lived here?"

"Yes, there have been what I suppose you'd call keepers. There's a small sitting area and kitchen with a separate place to sleep."

She smoothed her already smooth skirts and gazed at him through the sunlight. "Thank you for showing it to me."

He neared. "You're welcome. It's one of my favorite spots on the entire estate."

"I can see why," she replied breathlessly.

He closed the gap between them. He inhaled her scent of oranges and vanilla. At that moment, he thought it was the most intoxicating smell. She was so close, he could see the vein on her long, fine neck pulsing. Was she nervous? She didn't appear to be, but he knew she could keep her feelings bottled up inside for no one to see. He tucked his hand under her chin and bent his head.

And then he kissed her.

To his relief, she didn't pull back in shock. Instead, she stood there quietly, allowing him to take the lead. Her lips tasted of honey and tea as he ran his tongue along them. The urge for more consumed him as he parted her lips with his tongue. She opened to him, their kiss becoming more passionate and needy. Her arms wrapped around his neck, her fingers running through his hair.

Reluctantly, he broke the kiss, his breathing ragged. His cock was hard with need. The one thing he swore he'd never do was happening, and he didn't want it to end. He stared down at her, her lips swollen from his kiss. How long had it been since she'd kissed a man? Was he the first since her husband died?

Cupping her chin with his hand, he kissed her again. Again, she opened and responded to him. What started out as a simple kiss was now greedy and passionate. He wanted her like no other. Certainly, he'd kissed many a woman, but none of them aroused him the way Savannah did. He wanted to make love to her and claim her for his own.

"We must stop," he growled as he tore himself away.

"You brought me here to take advantage of me, Your Grace?"

"No, not at all. I've dreamt of kissing you. I merely got caught up in the moment. Forgive me."

She nodded, one hand absentmindedly touching her

hair. "There is nothing to forgive. It was as much my fault as it was yours, Your Grace."

"Gabriel. I asked you to call me Gabriel."

"Very well, Gabriel." She smiled. "What do we do now?"

"What do you want to do? We can either pretend that kiss never happened, or we can pursue our feelings."

The color rose in her cheeks. He wondered if they would flush when he finally bedded her. There was no doubt in his mind he was going to bed her and make her his, but then what?

"There is no way we can undo that kiss. I wouldn't want to, but there are others we have to think of."

"Vincent, yes. I understand." He smiled. "As far as Lady Dorset, I don't care what she thinks."

"She's still my mother-in-law."

"True, but she surely can't expect you to live out your days alone and unloved."

"I have Vincent," she whispered.

"Yes, and he always will love you. You must face the fact his life will be changing in the next few years. He will go off to school. Eventually university. He'll marry, have children of his own."

"But he'll always love me."

He ran his fingers along her cheek. "Is that enough? Are you willing to forsake a life of your own?"

"I would do anything for my son. Anything."

"I know."

He leaned over and kissed her once again. Savannah sighed as he did. "If we're going to do this, we must be discreet and go slowly. Can you do that for me?"

He arched a brow and nipped her lower lip with his teeth. "For you, I can do anything. I would move heaven and earth if it meant having you by my side."

· · ·

SHE WANTED him to kiss her. She wanted more. Her body ached for his touch, his kisses, for he was a most talented kisser. She imagined what sort of lover he'd be. Not that she had much experience. Roland had been her first and only, and he was attentive, but to him, it was a matter of marital duty. Once they married and he'd bedded her, he was like most husbands. He came to her for one thing and one thing only. Sex. She often wondered if he kept a mistress, given all the late nights he spent out. He'd always told her it was for business.

If she allowed this to go on, would Gabriel be the same way? Was he one of those men? She couldn't think of that. She needed to savor every moment with him and see where this all led.

Gabriel did have one distinct advantage over others, if there were to be others: he already had a genuine interest and fondness for Vincent, and her son adored Gabriel.

They were still standing on the roof, Gabriel's arms around her, when suddenly, he loosened his embrace.

"We need to head back." He pointed to a bank of dark clouds off on the horizon. "You see those? They'll be here before you know it and bring the rain."

He didn't say another word, just took her hand and led her down the stairs. It was cool and damp inside. The sun wasn't out to warm the tower.

As Gabriel was getting the horses, Savannah looked around the small rooms. It was certainly cramped, but one person, possibly two, could get by in here.

Hearing the sound of horses outside the door, she walked over and opened the door and was met by Gabriel, knowing from his heated gaze what was running through his mind. Would they even be compatible? It was easy to say they were this early on.

She had to make the right decision, and to do that, she needed time. Standing this close to him made her body scream with desire. Would she feel that once she was back at Sky View? Or would she go with the feeling he was a cad and would just use her? That she would simply be another in a long line of women who, like she, entered into a relationship with Gabriel only to be hurt and burned. If he hurt her, Savannah had no doubt she would be devastated beyond words.

CHAPTER 16

Savannah had just sat down with her needlework. The day was gray and rainy, just as Gabriel had predicted. Savannah sat in a chair near the long windows, sorting her threads, looking for a particular shade of green when the dowager countess entered the drawing room.

Lady Dorset placed her needlework basket next to her feet as she sat in a matching chair near Savannah. The older woman had not said anything about her outing with Gabriel the afternoon before. That was uncharacteristic of the dowager countess, as Savannah had learned. The woman always had something to say, even if her opinion was not required.

"You're spending a great amount of time with the duke."

"He's been most gracious showing me around the estate," she replied. She separated a green thread and placed the others back in the basket at her feet.

"I don't think you should pursue this silly notion you seem to have."

Savannah arched a brow and set the thread down. "And what silly notion would that be?"

"The idea you seem to have about landing the duke

as your husband. I can assure you, my dear, you are not duchess material."

"I have no such intentions. As he is Vincent's mentor, it is in our best interests that the two of us bond through some sort of friendship."

"No man can be just friends with a woman. It simply isn't done."

"I disagree." She picked up the needle she'd just threaded and began working. She needed some sort of distraction or she might say something she'd regret.

"Be that as it may, my dear. You don't need to be spending so much time with the duke."

"And if he invites me?"

"You'll decline, of course."

Savannah punched the needle through the fabric. "I'll do no such thing."

"You can and you will. The duke will never lower himself to court a commoner. And the less often the ton are reminded that Vincent's mother is an American, the better it will be for him."

Savannah threw her needlework into the basket. She could no longer bear to be in the same room as this horrid woman. She stormed out of the room, startling the footman standing on the other side of the door.

As she left, she thought she heard the dowager countess laughing.

She needed to do something with her mother-in-law. *Former* mother-in-law. While it was to her advantage to have the older woman residing in the manor house, it was all she could do to stand the woman's presence. Why didn't the dowager countess live in the dower house? She'd seen it from afar and had wondered why Lady Dorset didn't opt for a place of her own. Same as in London. Lady Dorset had a place of her own, but preferred what had been her son's. Lady Dorset was not one to give things up, at least not easily.

Savannah sat on the window seat in her small sitting room and stared out at the rain. It was pelting down against the windows, showing no signs of letting up. What was it about dark days like this that brought out the worst in people? At least it seemed that way today.

Discretion was needed in this situation. She needed to tread lightly. The countess would expect her to go directly to the duke and confide in him. What she would do instead would be to sit back and let the situation unfold. The countess would no doubt send him a missive outlining their disagreement, and she'd want him to hear it from her first. Let her. She would be playing right into Savannah's hands.

GABRIEL SAT BACK in the chair behind his desk and raised his feet. He disliked days such as these, dark and rainy, especially in the middle of summer. He'd finished going over the estate ledgers and noted there were only so many ways one could study the numbers. He shut his eyes and recalled the time he'd spent with Savannah.

She was a difficult woman to get to know. She kept her innermost thoughts to herself some of the time, but other times, she thought nothing more than to speak her mind. He tried to imagine her as a young wife in America. How had she and her late husband lived? She had never revealed much about what sort of husband his old friend was. Savannah had skirted the issue, telling him what she thought he wanted to hear.

Their conversation in the tower had been quite productive, or at least he thought it had. She was willing to see where a relationship might go so long as he didn't push the issue. His answer was yes, and he meant it. He'd move heaven and earth for this woman.

As much as he wanted to bed her, he would take as much time as she needed. The idea was strange to him. As a bachelor, women never were a problem. They threw themselves at his feet, and he could always find a willing partner for bed sports.

He stared down at a letter from his sister, Frannie, who lived in Cambridge with her husband, George, and two small girls, Vicki and Joan. He hadn't seen her in months, not since he'd made the journey to Cambridge.

Under Frannie's letter was one from Parr. The two of them were going to invest in two new ships, one that would make voyages to the Caribbean, while the other would go back and forth to America, and either he or Parr needed to make the long voyage to tie up ends on that side of the Atlantic. Parr had volunteered and was prepared to go as soon as loose ends were tied up.

Of the two ships, one was still at the shipyard in Southampton where final fittings were being made. The other sat in dry dock for a thorough maintenance. The latter had been negotiated during the purchase.

Parr would set sail for New York on the third ship they owned. While there, he would take care of the necessary paperwork. Though they had a reliable man on the ground there, Parr wanted to make sure everything was ready for when the ships docked in New York.

As soon as Parr finished in New York, he would make his way to Charleston or Savannah to inquire about procuring cotton, which was highly sought after.

He smiled. He realized once again how little he knew of her upbringing and childhood. It was not a matter she shared. Perhaps in time.

He picked up the letter from Parr, broke the seal, and read the words. He'd hired a former Bow Street runner to search for this mysterious man looking so much like Roland Dawson. Though he and Parr were convinced it wasn't their old friend come back from the dead, they both wanted to put Savannah's mind at ease.

Parr also indicated he would be arriving in a fortnight to discuss his upcoming trip to America and to do some hunting on Gabriel's estate. He welcomed his friend's visit. As usual during the summer months, visitors were plenty, which meant he would need to be a hospitable host and would have to inform his housekeeper of the additional guests. Mrs. White always went out of her way to make sure his guests were comfortable and had everything they needed.

Swinging his legs off the desk, he searched for a fresh sheet of paper. He wrote a missive to his sister telling her he'd love for her and her family to come visit and that he awaited her word on when they would arrive. His next was to Parr telling him he was awaiting his arrival.

He rang for the butler, who promptly entered the study. Sometimes Gabriel swore the man hovered outside wherever he was to see to his needs. Simmons was far too efficient, not to mention dedicated.

"See that these are disbursed today."

"Yes, Your Grace." Simmons held out a silver tray. "This just came for you and does not require a reply, Your Grace."

Gabriel took the missive and dismissed Simmons. "Thank you."

He waited until the door closed before reading the note. A feminine fragrance permeated his senses. The writing appeared to be that of a woman, but not one he recognized. Carefully, he opened the paper and read the words.

It was from Savannah. She wanted to meet with him

privately and, if the weather cleared, would meet him at the tower the following afternoon. She gave a time. Nothing else except that. He would have offered to come for her, but she had been insistent in her letter that they arrive separately.

He wondered why the mystery. What was going on that she needed to meet him alone? She was a widow, so she could do more than an unmarried woman might. The mystery intrigued him. He'd have to wait to find out until tomorrow, as sending a reply would be foolish. It was obvious she wanted no one to know of their meeting.

CHAPTER 17

Savannah waited nervously on her horse outside the tower. She hated being so clandestine about meeting Gabriel, but after her conversation with the dowager countess, she felt she was left with no choice. She needed answers to some of the claims Lady Dorset had made. She needed to hear it straight from Gabriel.

Certainly, she had never expected he would mentor Vincent for nothing. It was the tone and insinuations made by the countess that gave her pause. She also thought Gabriel should be made aware of Lady Dorset's demand that she shouldn't be spending so much time with him. Not that it was any of her business, but she knew the woman could make life miserable for her. Lady Dorset thought highly of Gabriel, and Savannah had no doubt the older woman would listen to him.

She thought warmly of Gabriel. The two of them had danced around any hint of a personal relationship between them. She was attracted to him, and for the first time found herself wanting more of him. She knew he felt the same by the way he stared at her with those emerald eyes. Eyes that longed for more than a simple afternoon of polite conversation. Certainly, as a widow, she could have an affair with Gabriel, but she wanted more. She wanted to share his bed and wake alongside him. She wanted to share their life together. Did she dare hope for that?

The day was perfect compared to the dark and rainy day experienced yesterday. Today the sun was out, and the sky was an amazing shade of blue with the occasional puffy white cloud floating by.

The bay gelding was restless, so she walked him around the tower as she waited on Gabriel. She had left the house and gone to the stables to have a horse saddled. The stable master was not happy when she insisted she didn't need someone to ride with her. He felt she didn't know the estate well enough to venture off on her own. Savannah was suspicious of the idea of one of the stable boys riding with her, afraid they would report back to the countess.

Which was why she had ridden off in the opposite direction of Brook Fall. After she was out of sight of the house and the stables, she doubled back on a trail and headed toward the tower.

Savannah waited nervously on her horse outside the tower when she heard the sounds of another approaching. She held her breath, hoping against hope it was Gabriel. A moment later, he appeared. She urged her horse toward his.

"Were you afraid I might not come?" he asked as he swung down off his stallion.

"No, though the thought had crossed my mind that someone might have intercepted my missive."

He arched a brow. "Why would someone do that?"

"Help me down from my horse, and I'll tell you what's going on."

He walked over and put his hands on her waist, then set her down on the ground. "Your missive said nothing, though I sensed urgency to it. Has something happened?"

"Walk with me," she said. As they walked along a pathway, she told him about her conversation with Lady Dorset. She found herself telling him everything. She wanted the truth, and if they didn't start being honest with each other now, there was no way they could forge a relationship.

He stopped and faced her. "Yes, it's true. All of it. You do know the dowager has no authority over the earldom's money. I didn't know about you except through what little Roland told me in the few letters he sent to me from America."

"Yes, I know. What I'm also discovering is I know less about my husband than I thought."

"It happens," Gabriel replied. "Men get caught up in business and take their wives for granted."

"True," she replied. "Do you have any suggestions on how I should handle Lady Dorset?" She wasn't upset he hadn't told her about any of this. He might not have known just how far the dowager had gone with what information she shared with her.

They began walking again. "There is a perfectly good dower house both here and in London. Have her move into what is her house."

"Do I even have the authority to do that?"

"As Vincent's mother, you can do far more than you think. Obviously, Lady Dorset hasn't bothered informing you."

"You mean I can act on Vincent's behalf?"

He nodded and slowed his gait. She figured he must have noticed she was having trouble keeping up with his longer strides. "Yes, to a point. That was part of the reason she came to me. He needs a male influence, one who understands the ways of the aristocracy."

"I have no problem with that, you know that."

"Such as the countess?"

She arched a brow. "She's an exception. I'm still afraid she's going to attempt to walk all over me and ignore my request that she move into the dower house."

"Give it a try. You're stronger than you think."

She smiled and locked eyes with him. "Very well. I'll sit her down and inform her of my decision. What if she claims I have no authority? As I've said, I'm only Vincent's mother."

"You're the mother of the Earl of Dorset, and you're acting on his behalf. If she gives you any problems after telling her that, let me know. I'll right the matter."

"Thank you again. I hate that we can't get along, or that she doesn't want to."

"Lady Dorset has always been somewhat difficult. She's just become worse since Timothy died."

"I'm sure it has to do with change. Both her sons died, and the earldom went to a grandson she'd never met. It has to be difficult."

He stopped next to a rowan tree that grew at the edge of the path. "I'm sure it is, but you must also never doubt yourself."

"I won't. I promise to suggest she move into the dower house. I'm sure the situation will present itself in no time."

Her intention had been to confront him about what exactly the countess had given him or had promised him. She would ask and see what his answer was, see if he would indeed tell her. She was so caught up in her own thoughts, she startled at Gabriel's presence as he tied their horses to a tree, then drew near and kissed her.

The kiss started out slow and sensual, two people discovering each other. As the kiss continued, the more passionate they both became. Savannah learned that

Gabriel was a bossy kisser. She felt as though he consumed her very being.

He pulled her closer to him, and she could feel the heat of his body as he backed her against the tree. She wound her arms around his neck, running her fingers through his golden hair as he pushed her legs apart with his.

She caught herself moaning as his hands pulled her against his hardened cock. She was losing control, her need of this man far greater than any vow she made to herself to dislike him. His hand slipped under her skirts and easily found her thigh. His touch was gentle as he explored what he hadn't before. Finally, he found what he was after and touched the cloth that separated her from his long fingers.

"You're wet," he growled. "What do you want?"

"You," she gasped, saying words she thought she'd never share with another man. "I want you to touch me, make love to me."

His tongue touched her skin, and she felt fire.

A kiss to the base of her neck sent a shiver of desire through her.

One hand came around her body and settled on the underside of her breast, aching and full. He lifted her breast in his hand and slowly and languidly rubbed his thumb over her nipple. His other hand came to join the first and lifted the opposite breast.

"Gabriel," she whispered, writhing against him. He pinched on nipple, and she gasped. "Please."

He nipped at her earlobe, sending pleasure soaring through her. "Come, let's go inside," he said.

Inside the tower, he pulled her to him, lifting her in his arms as he took her to the bed. He laid her down, letting her pull him to join her on the cotton coverlet. She kissed him, a long and lush kiss with a slow sweep of her tongue until they were both aching with need.

His fingertips lightly traced over her arm to her hip. She shivered with anticipation.

She began to strip him out of his coat and untied his cravat. Tossing the cravat away, her hands explored the fine linen of his shirt, until she pulled it away from his trousers.

He caught her chin in his fingers, tilting her face to his for another kiss.

He paused for a moment, one finger tracing the line of her jaw. "What do you need?"

"I need you. Now."

He began to unfasten her clothing, until piece by piece, she lay naked to him. Aching for him. He kissed her jaw, her neck, the slope of one shoulder, as her fingers slid into his hair, her back arching toward him, pressing her body closer to him.

His lips closed tightly around her nipple, and he sucked gently, working at her until she was fisting his hair and whispering his name. His hand slid over her hip, down the delicate skin of her thigh as he teased her legs apart until she was open to him. She lifted her hips to meet his touch, rocking against him. She ached with need for him.

She lifted her hips against him, pushing the hard length of him against her softness until they both groaned. "Make me yours," she breathlessly whispered.

He growled deep in this throat, then moved down her body, kissing her as he went until he was exactly where they both wanted him to be. She panted as he settled his lips to her, holding her wide, licking her in long, thick strokes.

"Yes," she sighed.

"I want you to touch yourself while I come," he said. She watched as he took himself in hand and stroked himself in time to her movements, the pleasure of her moving against him. Her thighs trembled and her fingers tightened in his hair as she found her climax, shouting his name as he worked her with his tongue until all she knew was her pleasure.

As the last ripple of pleasure coursed through her, he moved to lie beside her. Savannah, however, had other plans. She pushed him onto his back and climbed atop him. "You didn't come," she whispered.

"It was all for you," he said.

She ground her hips against him until he groaned. She sat back on his thighs and took him in hand. She grinned as she felt him suck in a breath when she touched him. She moved, rubbing against him until she felt his hand between them. She lifted herself, his tip settling at the opening of her hot, wet core She lowered herself onto him until she was impaled by his cock.

She kissed him, rocking into him until she found her rhythm. He thrust into her, moving deeper, faster, until she matched him thrust for thrust.

She slid a finger between them to find her pleasure again, her fingers working the heat of her need as he continued to thrust into her.

"Does that feel good?" he asked.

"Yes," she sighed. Suddenly, her eyes flew open and she cried out his name.

"Look at me as you take your pleasure."

She did until he followed her over the edge, shouting her name, drawing her orgasm out, refusing to stop until she was spent.

He turned onto his side, pulling her with him, her silken hair falling around her, their breaths still fast. They lay there in silence for a few moments, their bodies sated. In this one singular moment, this was perfection.

He stroked his hand down her bare skin, and she sighed. "I don't want this to end," she said.

"Neither do I."

"Do we dare?

"Dare what? Be happy? Yes, of course," he whispered in her ear.

"How?"

"It'll all work out my, love. You'll see."

~

HE RAN his hand over her skin once again, pulling her tight against him. This was what it was to be happy, to be loved. He knew what the future held. The two of them would marry, but not right away. They must have a respectable period of courtship. For Vincent to warm to the idea of his mother remarrying and a new man coming into his life permanently.

First, he needed to try to find this man who looked so much like Roland and put everyone's minds at ease. Finding him wouldn't be easy, but that was why his friend Parr thought they should hire a runner or two. He and Parr would discuss the matter, and he hoped the runners would have more luck than they had in finding this mysterious man.

If it was Roland, why come to England? Why risk being discovered by someone who knew him? He'd heard of men who abandoned their wives and families, leaving no trace of where they'd gone. Still, he couldn't imagine his friend doing something like that. Even if he were in some sort of trouble, he would have made contact with someone he knew. Found someone to help him.

Which was exactly why Gabriel didn't believe the man in question was, in fact, Roland Dawson. Roland was too much of a man to ever consider abandoning his wife and young son or his businesses. No, if this man were Roland, he would have connected with his family. He would also be the next earl.

"What are you thinking?" Savannah huskily asked him as she propped herself up on an elbow.

"Just how incredibly happy you've made me."

"Liar. Your mind was whirling around in thought."

He pulled her to him and kissed her. "True, but all good things."

"Such as?"

"How much I'm going to enjoy spoiling you, loving you."

She ran her delicate fingers through his chest hair. "Don't get ahead of yourself, Gabriel. There are others we must consider, such as Vincent."

"I know, and we will."

"As long as you understand that," she said, sitting up. "Now I must be getting back. I've been away far too long."

"I thought you weren't going to be ruled by the dowager countess."

"I'm not. It's simply that I don't wish to be late taking tea with Vincent. It's something I try to do every day."

"Very well. I can hardly compete with an up-and-coming young earl."

"Why don't you come to dinner? I believe Lady Dorset had plans for dinner with her friend Lady Eugenia. Her husband has gone to Yorkshire in the north to check on one of his lesser estates."

"I would love to."

She got off the bed and began gathering her clothes, handing him his as she came across them. The idea of spending the rest of his life with this magnificent creature made his cock harden. He pulled on his trousers and grinned.

"What's so funny?" she inquired.

"Nothing. Just that you've made me so incredibly happy."

"So you've said," she replied with a smirk.

~

GABRIEL WAS surprised when he arrived at Sky View for dinner and found Lady Dorset still at home. It immediately made him wonder if one of the countess's faithful servants might have been spying on them earlier in the day. He hadn't found signs of anyone following them, but simply the idea that Savannah went out alone and without a stable boy might have been enough for the dowager countess to cancel her plans for the evening.

"Lady Dorset, you look lovely as always," he murmured over her gloved hand.

"Your Grace." Her reply was short and to the point. By the way she stared at him and then at Savannah, he wondered if indeed they'd been caught.

It didn't matter one way or another if they had. He refused to hide his feelings. He'd done that for far too long. He wanted to shout his love for this woman from the rooftops. His feelings were so different from the way he'd been raised, where personal feelings were not to be displayed in public.

The dowager countess had been brought up in the same manner and had raised her own children to keep their feelings tucked away. She would probably have an apoplexy when she realized he wasn't going to follow those who went ahead of him. He was a duke, after all, and expected to maintain a certain decorum. Society looked up to him.

He shifted his attention to Savannah, who stood next to the fire with an expression of unease as she undoubtedly knew that whatever plans she might have had for them this evening had been thwarted by the countess.

"Thank you for coming, Your Grace."

"My pleasure," he replied. He kissed the back of Savannah's hand, not lingering too long as the countess was observant of their every move.

He followed the ladies' lead and sat on a cream-colored damask chair. He decided to break the tension in the room to help ease Savannah's discomfort.

"My sister Frannie and her family are coming for a visit."

"She's married to that Cambridge professor?" Lady Dorset asked. The countess knew that because she'd been invited to Frannie's wedding at Brook Fall some seven years prior.

"Yes," he tartly replied.

"I know you'll be happy to see her. Do you get to see her often?" Savannah asked.

"Once or twice a year. I try to make a trip to Cambridge if I'm in London for any length of time. She makes a point of visiting in the summer as well."

"His Grace has another sister, Henrietta, who's married to a Frenchman and living in the south of France," Lady Dorset said.

Gabriel nodded. "She lives in a town called Provence. Their home overlooks the Mediterranean Sea. It's quite beautiful."

"I've always wanted to see the Mediterranean. I understand it's the most beautiful hue of blue. Maybe someday I'll get to see France and Italy."

"You've never traveled far?" the countess asked.

"No, the farthest I'd been prior to coming to England was my mother's brother's plantation in Georgia. It isn't far from the coast, but the Atlantic hardly can compare with the Mediterranean for beauty."

Lady Dorset couldn't contain herself from pointing out how limited Americans were in their travel choices. "It must have been hard to grow up there with so few places to visit."

"Not at all. While America may not have the older cities, we do have places like Newport."

"My friend the Earl of Wexford says it's one of his favorite places to go when he visits," Gabriel added.

"It is beautiful in its own way."

Clearly bored with the conversation and not being the center of everyone's attention, Lady Dorset changed the subject. "Are you planning your annual summer house party this year?"

"I thought I'd wait until Frannie arrives and see if she'd like to help plan it. If she doesn't, I'll not have it this summer."

The countess nodded politely. "It is a feat having a house full of guests. If your sister decides she wants to hold it, I'd be happy to assist her in any of the arrangements."

"You're too kind, Lady Dorset. I'm sure Frannie would appreciate any assistance you could give her."

Not wanting the dowager duchess to reveal too much about his notorious house parties in front of Savannah, he instead inquired about young Vincent. That would be a discussion to have later with Savannah. "Has Vincent gotten to see the lake?"

"What lake?" Savannah asked. He hadn't taken her to it yet, preferring the solitude his own estate offered.

"It's a lake my late husband's grandfather had built to fish from."

"Vincent loves to fish!"

Gabriel already knew that because he and young Vincent had discussed it in great length during one of times Gabriel had called on the boy in an effort to get to know him.

"Then it's settled. I'll take him."

Lady Dorset clucked her tongue in disapproval. "I'm sure Your Grace has more pressing matters. If the boy wishes to learn to fish, one of the servants can teach him."

"Nonsense. I've been meaning to spend more time with him since you asked me to help ready the boy for his life's work."

He glanced at Savannah, who had a twinkle in her eye as she tried not to laugh. She held herself very much as an aristocratic lady would. The lavender gown she wore was accented with deep purple ribbon under her bust and on the sleeves. She was going to make a perfect duchess. His duchess.

"You might enjoy joining Vincent and me, Mrs. Dawson."

He watched intently as she found a way to answer. He enjoyed keeping her off balance. At least some of the time.

CHAPTER 18

Vincent's enthusiasm was infectious as Savannah and her son waited for the duke to arrive. Savannah had joined Vincent for breakfast, something she missed terribly, and gave him the news the duke would be calling on them to take them for a picnic. She hadn't mentioned the fishing part because she wanted to let Gabriel surprise him with that.

Savannah was grateful Lady Dorset rarely rose before noon. She didn't approve of Vincent missing time away from his studies and certainly wouldn't care for him running in and out of the drawing room as he found a window to look through as he watched for the duke. No, the dowager duchess believed children should be seen and not heard, and should only be seen once a day for no more than ten minutes. It spoiled them, she told Savannah on more than one occasion.

Though Roland adored his son, he too came from that school of thinking. He expected his son to take his studies seriously, and when he did spend time with Vincent in the evenings or at dinner, their conversations always revolved around what he'd learned that day or a topic of Roland's choosing. For a man so desperate to break his bonds with his stuffy English upbringing, he certainly expected nothing but the best from his young son.

Vincent ran into the drawing room, the footman unable to keep up with the youngster's constant comings and goings through the drawing room door.

"Mama, there's a wagon coming down the drive. Do you think the duke will be far behind?"

"I have no doubt he'll arrive any moment. He's probably driving that wagon."

Vincent sniffed like a young aristocrat. "Don't be silly, Mama. The duke would never be seen in anything but one of his carriages."

"He may have made an exception for you. How else would we get to where he's taking us?"

Her son rolled his eyes. "We could ride."

"That is true. Why don't you see where that wagon is now?"

He bolted out of the room. Savannah sighed, thinking of how much her son had changed over the past few months. The boy he'd once been had all but disappeared. Though he maintained a facade of seriousness, Vincent would forget and let the rambunctious young boy loose.

A few minutes later, he returned. This time, Gabriel followed, a corner of his mouth curved up. It was obvious he enjoyed spending time with Vincent. Without fail, he always brought something with him for the boy. The two were bonding, Vincent and the duke would have nonstop conversations about whatever caught her son's interest. It didn't matter if the subject matter was childish or boring to an adult, Gabriel would listen attentively, contributing to the conversation as was appropriate.

"Mama, it was the duke in the wagon!"

"So it was," she replied, smiling at Gabriel.

"Good morning, Mrs. Dawson," he said. His hair

was already disheveled, a stray lock charmingly covering one eye. "I took the liberty of having my cook prepare a luncheon for us, which is why I needed the wagon." He winked at Savannah, then turned his attention to Vincent.

"Where are we going, Your Grace?" Vincent asked.

"I thought perhaps you'd like to go fishing. There is a lake I'm going to take you and your mother to. You and I can fish."

"Are you sure there are fish in this lake? Sometimes lakes have no fish."

"I can assure you, Master Vincent, this lake has plenty of fish. Your father, uncle, and I used to fish there quite regularly when we were home for the summer."

Satisfied with Gabriel's answers, Vincent ran in front of them to the drawing room door. "Come on!"

Gabriel chuckled and turned to Savannah. "I believe he's excited. If you're ready, we'll be on our way."

"Yes, let's, or Vincent won't quit pestering us until we're in that wagon and on our way."

Vincent was a nonstop bundle of energy, running up and down the stone stairs to the house, prodding his mother and Gabriel to walk faster. After making sure Vincent was put into the back for the ride, the duke helped Savannah into the wagon. Vincent had let it be known he wasn't going to ride in the front with two adults on either side. He was not a baby and refused to be treated as one. Savannah had to hide a smile when her son made that announcement.

"I enjoyed last evening, even if Lady Dorset was there," he remarked once they were all settled.

"I did too." She smiled and stared up at the blue sky. It was one of those rare, perfect English summer days. Blue sky dotted with the occasional puffy white cloud, a slight breeze in the air. "I suspect she canceled her plans once she heard you were coming for dinner."

"I thought as much. So you haven't been able to speak with her about moving into the dower house?"

"Trust me, Gabriel, when I have that conversation with her, you'll probably be able to hear her reply all the way to your house. That's how insulted she's going to act."

He smiled and focused on the horses and the path leading to the lake. "I'm afraid you're right about that."

"I don't understand her. One would think she'd be ecstatic to have her own household as she did when she was lady of the house."

"The blame lies with Timothy. He allowed her to stay on and manage the household after the earl died."

"Well, I plan to talk with her as soon as I can."

They were interrupted by Vincent, who had caught a glimpse of the lake as it came into view. "Look at the size of the lake! There must be lots of fish in it."

"It is beautiful. Pity the dowager countess doesn't make use of it."

Gabriel nodded. "It is beautiful, but Lady Dorset has never liked it, and unfortunately, it shows."

The grass was overgrown. It would take gardeners a solid day to even bring the place back. It appeared as though it hadn't been used in years.

"I plan to change that," Gabriel said. "It's too beautiful a spot to be allowed to sit in ruins. I'll speak with the master gardener about sending men down to mow and clean it up."

"Thank you." Savannah smiled at him.

Due to his enthusiasm, Vincent had to be reminded not to jump out of the wagon while it was coming to a stop. When Gabriel did bring the wagon to a halt, Vincent was the first one out, jumping out the back. The first place he took off to was the shoreline.

Savannah inhaled, holding her breath as she watched Vincent playing next to the water. She felt the gentle touch of Gabriel's hand on hers. "He's fine. Boys simply need to explore."

"I know, but I've never allowed him too close to water before."

"I'm here. I'll supervise him. He'll be fine, Savannah."

"I'm being silly, I know."

He shook his head. "No, you're not."

After jumping out of the wagon, Gabriel helped Savannah to the ground. His hands encircled her waist, and for a moment, she flushed at his touch. Gabriel felt it too as it took him a moment to release her. She was sure if Vincent had not been present, he might have kissed her.

He walked to the back of the wagon and removed a blanket and a basket, then led Savannah to an old oak tree. He spread the blanket out before removing his jacket and rolling up the sleeves of his white shirt.

"Are you going to be all right here?"

She smiled and nodded. "Oh yes. I'm looking forward to the two of you fishing. Or at least you fishing. I'm afraid Vincent's going to be too excited to stand still."

He cast his gaze over to the shore, where Vincent stood throwing stones into the lake.

"If he keeps throwing stones into the water, he's going to scare off all the fish," he said with a lopsided grin. "But that's part of being a young boy, too, I suppose."

"Yes, young boys are all about stones, sticks, and things like frogs and fish."

Before he could answer, Vincent came running up to them. "Can we fish now, Your Grace?"

Gabriel chuckled and tousled the young boy's hair. "Yes. Let's get our poles from the wagon. Worms too."

"You've got worms and poles?" He turned to his mother. "Did you hear that, Mama? His Grace brought poles to fish and worms too."

"Yes, I heard."

Gabriel began to walk back toward the wagon. "Come, Vincent. Your mother will watch, and remember, we must be quiet, or we'll scare the fish away."

The youngster nodded and skipped ahead of Gabriel toward the wagon and his fishing pole. Savannah watched the pair from her vantage point under the tree. She wondered how long she and Gabriel were going to have for their clandestine meetings. The dowager duchess probably had servants watching them, but how would Lady Dorset continue once she was asked to move to the dower house, a talk she'd yet to be able to have with the countess? She probably had loyal servants who, while they stayed behind in the main house, would continue to spy for her. Which was exactly why she needed to quit allowing the servants to run to Lady Dorset instead of her. She was the earl's mother and had more leverage than she chose to use. Yes, she needed to have that talk with the dowager countess. Things wouldn't be right until she did.

The day had presented itself much like it had when she met Gabriel at the tower. She leaned against the oak tree and watched in amusement as Vincent walked next to Gabriel, proudly carrying his fishing pole.

For a brief moment, she wondered what it would have been like if Roland were still alive. Would he have taken the time to teach his son, or would he have left it to others? Vincent had been only five when his father died, still too young for some things. She would like to think he would have done just as Gabriel was doing and would take Vincent to the river that ran near their house and showed his young son how to fish.

Gabriel was bent down, explaining the art of fishing. She was sure he would have a thousand questions for him. Vincent loved to talk, especially to Gabriel, and it would prove interesting to see whether he would be able to be quiet.

She marveled at how patient Gabriel was with him. Roland had trouble with that, especially when he was tired, which was one of the reasons he believed children should be seen and not heard.

Savannah sighed. She'd always wanted Vincent to have a brother or sister, but it never happened. Did she dare let her mind wander, to daydream about where her fledgling relationship with Gabriel might end up? Would he ask her to become his duchess, or would their relationship simply fall back into the comfortable, warm feeling of them just being friends? He was the talk of the ton. Women practically threw themselves at his feet. Every one of them wanted to become the next duchess of Clevedon. She herself didn't care about his title. She was drawn to the man. In spite of his reputation of being a rakehell and scoundrel, he was also known for his kind and giving spirit. As annoying as she had originally found him, Savannah still felt herself drawn to the real man. The one he revealed only to close friends and family.

She waved at Vincent, who, standing next to Gabriel, proudly showed off a worm he was holding in his hand. This experience would be forever embedded in her son's mind. His life had changed so radically since moving to England that it was the little things like learning how to put a worm on a hook that made it all worthwhile.

The two stood at the water's edge, each with a pole and trying to catch an elusive fish. As he was a seven-year-old boy, Vincent's mind soon moved on to other things. He fidgeted, struggling to stand still like Gabriel. Soon Gabriel said something to him, and Vincent pulled the line out of the water, dragging it behind him as he turned and headed in Savannah's direction.

"The fish don't like the worms, so His Grace said we should eat lunch," Vincent announced.

He started toward the basket, anxious to open it and see what Cook had packed for him. Savannah quietly reprimanded him, reminding him that he should help Gabriel with their fishing equipment.

As he went scurrying back to Gabriel, Savannah opened the basket and began pulling out their meal. Roasted chicken, apples and pears, along with bread and cheese would make for excellent fare. Lemonade for Vincent and a bottle of wine for the adults.

She began to put food onto a plate for Vincent when he quite adamantly reminded her he was able to do it for himself. She smiled and handed him a plate as Gabriel sat on the blanket.

"Vincent says there aren't any fish?"

"They're there. We'll try again after we've eaten." He winked at her and poured her a glass of wine as she finished making sure Vincent was taken care of.

"You have more patience than I would have thought."

A few minutes later, with most of his meal finished and growing restless, Vincent asked his mother if he could explore. After she told him to stay where she and Gabriel could see him, he scampered off leaving the two adults on their own.

"You're quite beautiful," Gabriel said as he poured them both another glass of wine. "That color becomes you."

Savannah glanced down at the pale yellow day dress she'd chosen to wear and smiled. "Thank you."

A moment passed in silence.

"My sister Frannie should be here soon."

"Yes, and I'm sure you'll be happy to see her."

"Yes, I will, except for the times she gets on me about finding a wife. Which she seems to do at least once every time she visits."

Savannah smiled. "It sounds like she worries about her brother."

"Needlessly."

"Says the handsome single gentleman."

This time, he threw his head back and laughed. It came from deep in his chest, and Savannah found she rather liked hearing him laugh. "The two of you ought to get along quite well."

"You wish me to meet your family?"

"Of course I do. I want to introduce you to everyone I know. I thought you understood the feelings I have for you. They're not fleeting, Savannah."

"I know."

"Then what's the problem?" He reached out and tucked a stray strand of hair behind her ear.

"I'm feeling out of my depth here in England, and you're a man of means, while I'm a nobody."

He arched a brow. "You're somebody to me."

She shifted her gaze from him. "I also never gave much thought to ever meeting another man to take Roland's place, so I'm still a bit startled about it."

"You mean you've never given thought to re-marrying?"

She nodded and smiled. "Yes, that's exactly what I mean."

"Perhaps I need to be a little more transparent about courting you."

She felt herself once again feeling hot and flushed at his words. It was as though she were a schoolgirl and not a woman who'd lost her husband. This man was truly serious about courting her, and she had no intention of ruining it. He was a good man, and she wouldn't find a better husband or father for Vincent.

She gazed around, searching for her mischievous son. Her face must have shown panic when he was nowhere to be found, because Gabriel squeezed her hand and rose to his feet.

"I'm sure he's close," he assured her as he began searching for her son. He called out to Vincent, and not hearing a response, Savannah jumped to her feet to join him.

After a few minutes of calling and searching, Gabriel found him at the water's edge trying to catch a frog. Startled, Vincent fell back into the sand, and the frog jumped off, out of sight.

"He's right here," he called to Savannah.

She came running, and as much as she didn't want to scold the boy in front of Gabriel, she couldn't help herself. "Don't you scare me like that. Weren't you told to stay in sight?"

"Yes, ma'am."

She bid him to go sit on the blanket while she regained her composure.

"He's just a boy. I'm sure he meant no harm. He was chasing a frog," Gabriel said softly.

"Which is fine, except that he was practically in the water. He doesn't know how to swim, Gabriel."

"Then we'll teach him."

"Teach him? You and me?"

"Yes. We can come another day, and I'll start teaching him."

She nodded and smoothed her dress. "Thank you."

He cupped her chin. "You don't need to thank me." His lips found hers, and she kissed him back, until she realized Vincent could see them.

She slowly pulled away. "We shouldn't. Not in front of Vincent. Not yet."

"We need to talk with him about all this."

"Agreed, but you know how excited he is about you

spending time with us. I'm afraid he'll blurt something out in front of his grandmother."

He smiled and led her back to the blanket, where Vincent was waiting on them. "I believe there's a piece of chocolate cake in the basket, Vincent."

His eyes lit up, and he leapt toward the basket. Once he got settled with his dessert, Savannah scolded him, just enough for him to know he'd scared her.

"You know better than to play around water."

He nodded, and Gabriel joined in. "I'm going to teach you to swim."

"You are?"

"Yes. We'll begin in the next day or two. Do you think you're up to it?"

"I am!" he crowed.

A short time later, Savannah had everything packed back in the basket. She folded the blanket and watched as Gabriel and Vincent tried one more time to hook a fish, without success.

Vincent fell asleep on the way back to the house, tired from the hours spent outside. The adults talked quietly between themselves as Gabriel maneuvered the wagon over sometimes rough terrain.

"It's been a lovely day, Gabriel. I hate to see it end."

He covered her hand with his as the manor house came into view. "It doesn't have to end. Join me for dinner. I'll send my carriage for you."

"Are you sure?"

"Of course I'm sure."

Gabriel brought the bays to a halt, and he had just jumped down to help Savannah descend from the wagon when he heard her scream. Alarmed, he put his hands on her waist and helped her down. All the time, she pointed at the stairs and the man coming toward them.

"Roland?" Savannah asked breathlessly, while Gabriel steadied her.

The man certainly appeared to be Roland Dawson. He had the same hair color as Vincent, light brown, and the Dawson blue eyes. Gabriel's instinct kicked in, and he was about to ask a question of Savannah.

That's when Savannah fainted in his arms.

CHAPTER 19

"*I* apologize," the stranger said as he approached. "I don't usually have that effect on people."

"You must be Roland and Timothy's cousin," Gabriel surmised as he carried Savannah toward the stairs and into the house. "See that Vincent is taken to the nursery—without seeing Mr....Mr.?" he barked to the footman standing around in disbelief.

"Dawson, Mortimer Dawson, and yes, I am their cousin."

Lady Dorset appeared at the door. "Oh my," she said. "I see you've met Mortimer." Her eyes twinkled with sinister glee.

Ignoring the dowager countess, Gabriel pushed past her and up the stairs to the drawing room, where he carefully set Savannah down on a settee. She was coming to, and squatting next to her, Gabriel patted her gloved hand.

"Savannah."

"What? Did I fall asleep? I had a dream or something. I thought Roland was here." Her voice was low and weak.

"Remember you telling me about seeing a man in

London you thought looked like Roland? Well, he is here. He's a cousin."

She opened her eyes wider and put her hand on her forehead. "So my mind wasn't playing tricks on me?"

"No, not at all."

"Vincent. He must be so confused. Where is he?"

"A footman took him inside through the kitchen. He didn't see anything," he assured her. "Let me get you a glass of sherry. It might help calm you."

She nodded and started to sit up on the gold damask settee. Gabriel offered his hand and helped her before walking across the room to a sideboard containing crystal decanters. He began to pick the sherry up, but was interrupted.

"Whiskey," Savannah whispered loudly.

He arched a brow and smiled before turning back around to pour her a finger of whiskey. He passed it to her and watched as she took a swallow.

"Aren't you going to join me?"

"No, not right now," he replied.

Gabriel snarled as Mortimer and Lady Dorset burst into the room, the poor footman looking apologetic.

"We came to see if Mrs. Dawson has recovered," Lady Dorset said smugly.

"I'm fine," Savannah murmured, staring at her husband's cousin. "Mr. Dawson merely caught me off guard. I didn't know you were to visit, sir."

Mortimer smiled warmly. "It was last-minute. I wrote Lady Dorset and told her I was in England for a short time and should like to visit."

Gabriel cocked a brow at the man. "So you don't actually live in England?"

"No. I work for the Crown in India. They send me home every couple of years or so, and this is the time."

Though he wanted to know more about what the man actually did for the crown, now was not the time.

Obviously, he was here to stay—at least for a few days.

"How long have you lived there?" Gabriel asked.

"Almost six years. This is my first time back," he replied. He looked at Gabriel curiously. "I'm sorry, but I don't believe we've met."

"Gabriel Armstrong, Duke of Clevedon," he said sharply.

The man nodded before turning to Savannah. "Lady Dorset had, of course, told me about Roland and Timothy. You have my deepest condolences, Mrs. Dawson."

"Thank you."

"You've been in England some time. Why is it you've just now come to visit?" Gabriel asked.

"I had business matters I had to attend to before I could break away from London."

Gabriel was curious as to what sort of business the man might have, since he seriously doubted any matters involving his job would be take place near the park, which was where Savannah had seen him.

He would contact Parr. He was still in London, and he could have the runners they'd hired look into this man's comings and goings since arriving back in England. Something about what he told him didn't ring right with him. There was something about him that set Gabriel on edge.

Savannah rose from the settee, and immediately he went to her side, concerned she wasn't fully recovered from her shock.

"If you all would excuse me, I believe I'd like to lie down for a while."

"Of course," Mortimer replied.

"I think that would be best. Should I still send my carriage for you?"

She nodded, but as usual, Lady Dorset had something to say. "I'm sorry, Your Grace, but Mrs. Dawson really can't abandon our guest on his first evening. Perhaps you'd care to join us, Your Grace?"

He gave Mortimer a short bow. "I would indeed. I will enjoy hearing your stories about India."

Savannah smiled at him as though trying to apologize for their plans taking a sudden turn. "Then I look forward to seeing you this evening, Your Grace."

She nodded at the dowager countess and the interloper before leaving the room. He noticed she tried not to spend too much time staring at Dawson, imagining seeing someone who so closely resembled her late husband had to be unnerving. He wondered how the dowager countess felt about it, but then she had changed since losing both her sons, and he hadn't decided if it were for the better or not.

"Tea, Your Grace?" he heard the dowager countess ask from across the room.

He turned to face her. She watched him intently. "Thank you, but I must decline this time. I have some matters requiring my attention at home. I'll see you this evening."

He nodded in Dawson's direction before quitting the room. The important matter he needed to attend to was writing a letter to Parr and sending it to London. Between Parr, the Bow Street runners, and his contacts through Parliament, he would find out exactly who this Dawson fellow was and what he was up to.

SAVANNAH WAS RELIEVED when dinner was finished later that evening. Dinner had been a lively affair, filled mainly with Mortimer telling stories of his time in India. Some of it had fascinated her, while other stories he told made her grateful she lived in such a civilized country.

Questions had come to her since meeting her late husband's cousin, someone he never bothered to mention by name in the entire time they'd been together. She found that fact interesting, thinking there must be a story behind it.

While the men took their port and cigars in the dining room, Savannah thought to ask some questions about Mortimer as she and Lady Dorset had their tea.

"Don't you find Mortimer fascinating? All the places and things he's seen while in India amaze me," the older woman gushed. She accepted a cup of tea from Savannah as she wanted to break her daughter-in-law of the bad habits Americans had in regard to tea.

"I'm not sure fascinating is how I would describe him. He certainly likes to throw names about and mention how important he is to the Crown."

"You must learn to ignore certain aspects of Mortimer's personality, my dear. He's always been a bit eccentric."

Savannah arched a brow in the woman's direction. "You know what I find interesting?"

Lady Dorset sighed. "What, my dear?"

"That Roland never, in the entire time we were together, ever mention he even had a cousin named Mortimer. Why would he omit that?"

"I'm sure being that far away from home, it merely slipped Roland's mind. I mean, what were the chances you two would ever meet?"

She wasn't convinced, and she was certain Gabriel wasn't either. Since the man favored Roland so much, there was no room to believe he could be an imposter. So what was his true story?

Savannah took a sip of tea and put the cup down on the table beside her. "I also didn't know that your husband had a brother. Roland never mentioned his uncle either."

Lady Dorset waved her hand. "Roland was always disillusioned by the reality of our family, and he wasn't content with his role either."

"You mean his role as second son, the one who was the spare heir in case the earl never had children of his own."

"Correct." Her answer was curt.

"He never gave me the impression of wanting the earldom. It was part of the reason he came to America. To strike out on his own."

"Well, I could never see Roland joining the clergy or military. He didn't have the stomach for either."

"I have to agree with you there," Savannah replied.

The older woman apparently decided she was tired of talking about her husband's family, because she made an abrupt change to the course of their conversation. Savannah wondered if Gabriel was having any more luck than she was in the dining room.

"How was your little picnic with young Vincent and the duke?"

"How did you know we had a picnic?"

"The duke is far too caring and generous. He would never invite you along without one, else he and Vincent could have gone alone."

"Lady Dorset, your imagination is running wild tonight."

She shook her head. "No, not at all. I know all about your clandestine rendezvous at the tower. You went there for one purpose in mind. To make the duke your lover."

Savannah was astounded. How had she even known about this? It would have taken planning to know where and when the meeting was to take place. The more she thought about it, the angrier she got.

"What the duke and I do is none of your affair, madam."

Lady Dorset grimaced. "It is if it concerns my grandson."

"Madam, it is time for you to move into the dower house. I've been putting off having this conversation hoping you and I would at least find some middle ground, but you leave me no choice. Tomorrow, the house will be opened and made ready for you. I expect you to move out by week's end." Savannah was shaking, and she couldn't let Lady Dorset see that. She refused to be intimidated and mocked by this woman.

"I'm afraid you have no authority."

"That's where you're wrong. As the earl's mother, I may act on his behalf."

"The duke will never allow it."

"He oversees Vincent's transition and education so that when he's grown, he'll be the best earl." Lady Dorset began to speak, but Savannah continued. "I also know the duke oversees the earldom's affairs, making sure the estates and other interests continue to grow and thrive."

"It's going to take more than the command of some gel like you for me to move into that house."

Savannah shook her head. "You can make this easy, or you can make this hard. Either way, you're moving into the dower house. The one in London will be readied for you as well."

Lady Dorset rose from her chair and peered down at Savannah. "We'll just see about that." She began to walk out of the room in a huff just as the gentlemen returned from their port and cigars.

"Lady Dorset, would you care to play a game or two of whist?" Gabriel politely asked her.

She shook her head and sniffed. "I'm afraid I've developed a headache. I think I should retire for the night. Good night, Your Grace."

"Madam," he replied and bowed, watching her leave without a word.

He glanced at Savannah, who said nothing and tried to keep her upset with Lady Dorset from her expression. She would tell him of her conversation later, when Mortimer wasn't there to overhear. He must have felt as though he were intruding.

"It's been a long day for me as well. I believe I'll retire," Mortimer said. He turned to Savannah. "Mrs. Dawson. I look forward to hearing more about America. I've always found it a fascinating place, somewhere I hope to someday visit."

He bid Gabriel good night before quitting the room. Once the door closed behind him, Savannah breathed a sigh of relief.

"I sensed things were a bit tense between you and Lady Dorset?"

"You have no idea. She has been informed that both dower houses here and in London are being opened and made ready for her."

He smiled wickedly. "I take it she didn't approve?"

"You're being far too nice, Gabriel. She's refused to move."

She told him about the conversation the two had had earlier as Gabriel sat next to her on a settee and listened. He was having fun with this. Too much. Gabriel leaned over and kissed her on the neck.

"Gabriel, please. She has spies among the staff everywhere. She knows everywhere I go and what I do."

He sat up, eyebrow arched, his entire facial expression changed. "All the more reason for her to move out."

"That won't put an end to it if she has servants spying for her. They'll still do it regardless of whether she lives here or not."

"I'll put an end to it—that is if you'd like for me to speak with Higgins. I'm sure he knows who among the staff might be more likely to do the dowager countess's bidding."

"Can you?"

He nodded. "Of course I can. With my connection to Vincent, I certainly can. He's my charge and under my protection, as are you."

Savannah smiled demurely. "I was hoping you'd be able to handle this. I still feel like an outsider."

"You're not, and once Lady Dorset is moved into the dower house, you'll have better control of the household. She's been in charge far too long, and with you here, she knew it was just a matter of time before that was taken away from her."

"Thank you, Gabriel."

"You might also give some thought to sending Vincent to a boarding school in the autumn. I can make some inquiries if you like."

"But I thought we would wait at least a year?"

He patted her hand. "We can, but with the countess's anger over being forced out of the house, it might be best to move Vincent away from it."

Savannah shook her head. "Sending him to school might be just what she wants. He wouldn't be here, and it would be harder for me to keep track of who visits him. There must be another way."

"There is."

"What? Please tell me, Gabriel."

"I need some time to work everything out. We'll talk about it another time."

She knew exactly what he was trying to tell her without saying it out loud. If there were spies among the staff, sitting there in the drawing room was not the perfect place to have personal conversations.

"As you wish."

"Since we have no one to play cards with us, would you care for a game or two of cribbage?"

"I don't know. I'm not that good at it."

"Practice makes perfect," he replied with another of his smiles.

"Very well. Let me get it. We'll use that table," she said, pointing at a small square oak table on the far side of the room.

"I'll pour us a sherry."

She laughed at his suggestion, knowing he detested sherry. She knew this not because he'd told her, but because of the face he made whenever he consumed a glass. "I know you're not fond of sherry. Pour us a brandy. I believe you'll find a decanter on the sideboard with the others."

"I didn't know I was that obvious."

"Oh yes, it's quite obvious you're not fond of it."

She found the cribbage board in a drawer near the table they were planning on using. Setting it down on the table, she lowered herself to the chair and waited for Gabriel to bring the brandy. She watched him and smiled to herself. His face appeared rough, as though he needed a shave, and a rather large lock of hair had fallen down on his brow. He made no attempt to move it out of the way. Secretly, she wished he'd remove his jacket so she could admire his forearms if he rolled up his sleeves.

He brought two snifters across the room with him and set one in front of her, the other across from here, where he sat and settled in.

"So what did you think of your husband's cousin, Mortimer?"

"I cannot be sure. You men tend to act one way around women. I just felt he was being polite and observing everyone."

"Hmm, I believe you're right. I thought he was a

little out of line with some of the questions he asked while we were having our port. Then again, I suppose he's trying to be polite and catch up on family."

Savannah picked up her snifter and swirled the amber liquid. "I'm curious as to why now. Why, after all these years, he's taking a sudden interest in family."

"I thought the same thing, and I will still have him checked out."

They played several lively games of cribbage before Gabriel noted the late hour. "I should be leaving. It's late."

"I've thoroughly enjoyed the evening. Especially this part."

He reached across the table and took her hand. "I'm sorry you had to go through that with the countess. She is known for being blunt."

"I survived. Now that I've asked her to move into the dower house, I'm afraid she's going to be more difficult than usual."

"Remember I'm here if you need me."

She graced him with a smile. "I know, and I appreciate it. Really, I do."

"I'd best go. It's late."

He leaned in and kissed her gently. She kissed him back. She laughed softly in the back of her throat as the kiss continued.

He growled and lifted her off her feet. They stumbled against the wall, entwined and breathless as he pressed her body against him. She broke the kiss and laid her head on his shoulder. Heaven. She had found heaven when she was least searching for it.

CHAPTER 20

Savannah was tending a bed of roses in the garden outside the drawing room. She'd always loved gardening in America and needed to find an outlet here. She promised the horrified gardener she would confine her skills to this one bed, and if he found her work unsatisfactory to tell her, and she would stop.

The late-morning weather was perfect for being outside. It hadn't gotten too hot, and there was a breeze that would pop up now and then.

She was pruning dead blooms off a bush when Mortimer approached her. It wasn't that she didn't like her late husband's cousin; it was simply that she couldn't look at him without seeing Roland.

"I'm surprised to see you outside digging in the dirt," he said, stopping to admire another bush.

"Why should it surprise you? Many women are quite good at it."

He smiled. "I'm sure you're right."

"If you must know, I had to promise the gardener I wouldn't venture past this one bed. Poor man seemed horrified I would get my hands dirty."

He nodded. "I'm sure he's not used to ladies in his domain," he replied. "The reason I've come and sought you out is I wanted to see if you might be interested in riding into the village with me. There are some things I need to purchase, and I could use the company."

"I'm afraid I've already made plans." She studied him for a moment. She planned to ride to the castle. She had voiced her interest in touring an actual castle, and Gabriel had been amendable to showing her around. She planned to ride rather than having a carriage pre-pared and second, she thought it was no one's business where she went.

"Another time, then," he said, obviously disap-pointed.

She smiled and cut off the dead bloom. "I'm sure you'll find the village to your liking."

"No doubt I will. I haven't been since I was a child, and it's changed little since then."

She arched a brow. She was curious about his back-ground. "Did you live close by?"

He shook his head. "No, we lived two villages over. During the summer, however, my parents would let me spend a fortnight, sometimes more, with Roland and Timothy as I had no siblings."

"Ah yes, that makes perfect sense. It must have been lonely for you growing up alone."

"It was, especially during the summer as my father wouldn't allow me to wander too far from home."

"Understandable. Are your parents still living?"

"Yes. I plan to see them before I leave for India."

She walked to another bush, the last she was going to clean up today. Mortimer followed. "I'm sure your mother will be quite delighted to see you."

"She'll enjoy the diversion from taking care of my father as he's not in the best of health. His mind has begun to go, and I know from her letters, this distresses her the most."

"He doesn't always know who she is?"

He nodded. "No, and I'm afraid he's getting worse, making it harder for her to take care of him."

"Surely she could hire a nurse or some sort of companion to help her?"

"If my father hasn't gambled everything away."

"Surely not. He can't be in a position to go into the village and game." For a second, she felt almost sorry for Mortimer. He lived so far away, leaving the burden on his mother. She wondered what he would find. When was he planning on going?

"I'll find out. Unfortunately, the damage was done before his mind began fading. The only saving grace might be that my mother's brother took care of matters of the estate, and I hope he kept some money set aside for my mother. If not, I'm uncertain what the future holds.

"I'm sorry, though grateful your parents have a champion in their corner."

"Yes." He stood there for a moment, studying her. She could feel his blue eyes watching her. "I'm going to go. Perhaps another time you'll join me for a ride."

"Yes, of course," she replied without committing. His entire situation was quite unsettling. Roland had never made mention of his cousin, let alone the problems the family faced. Why? Why keep this a secret?

She stood and watched as his figure retreated out of sight before walking back to the house to change her clothes. As far as anyone would be concerned, she was going out riding. It wasn't unusual except for the fact she would be going alone as she went to meet with Gabriel.

This time, they would be meeting at his residence rather than the tower. She felt uncomfortable meeting him there since she learned the dowager countess obviously had her being watched. Gabriel had assured her she would be safe at his home, and he would send a man to meet her on the path where the two estates met.

She chose a dark blue riding outfit and, examining herself one last time in the looking glass, decided she'd made the right choice. Norma hadn't asked her where she was going to ride, and it caused Savannah to wonder. Did her maid know? Was she one of the dowager countess's spies? She doubted the former. Norma seemed to have no stomach for some of Lady Dorset's shenanigans. But did her maid know she was meeting the duke? She detested feeling paranoid in her own house, but since her discussion with the countess the night before, she was left with no choice.

"I thought I'd wear the rose-colored gown this evening, if you would make sure it's ready," she told Norma, who was walking toward the dressing room with the dress Savannah had just been wearing.

"Yes, ma'am. That is one of my favorites, if you don't mind my saying."

"Mine as well. It's not a color I would normally choose."

The maid bobbed her head in agreement and disappeared, leaving Savannah to wonder even more. She shook it off and headed out of the house to where a stable boy stood with her mount. She walked to the mounting block and settled herself on the animal.

She turned her horse in the opposite direction of where she was actually going. Gabriel had told her to do that and how to get to his manor house without being seen by anyone. This was crazy, but even Gabriel was uncomfortable with the fact someone might be keeping an eye on them. He agreed it was probably the dowager countess, but until he or one of his men could confront her, he told Savannah to lay low.

Finally, she met up with one of Gabriel's stable boys in a grove of trees. The weather was proving to be typical for English summer weather. For the first time in several days, the clouds had rolled in, threatening rain. Just as she thought it would rain, the sun came through a bank of clouds.

She followed the boy until the castle came into view. As she entered what had once been the bailey, she caught a glimpse of Gabriel coming to greet her. She rode her horse to his side and let him help her down.

"Did you have any problems?" He asked.

"No, none, but let's go in so we can speak in private."

He arched a brow but said nothing, instead leading her to a massive oak door. He led her to the library, where he closed the door behind them. "What's wrong?"

"It's probably nothing, but Norma seemed to be acting a bit off this morning."

"What do you mean?" he asked as he helped her to a deep red settee.

"She didn't ask where I was off to, which she usually always does, and wouldn't look me in the eye. I found it quite unnerving."

He smiled. "It might be because I sent for Higgins very early this morning. I told him what was amiss with Lady Dorset and the plan to have her move into the dower house. Then I mentioned the fact someone was reporting back to her, telling her everything going on with you."

"That makes sense, then, and explains why Norma was acting as she was."

"Higgins and I agreed it might take care of the matter, but we also figure it'll draw out whoever this person is."

"You don't think they'll stop?"

"No. They might lay low for a few days, but no."

"We can only hope for the best," she replied.

"Higgins is also going to ready the dower house for Lady Dorset."

"That's all well and good, but I still don't think she'll go without a fuss."

He sat next to her and took her hand. "It's a start. Hopefully, once she's moved in, she'll begin to enjoy having her own residence."

"I hope you're right," she said. "Oh, I almost forgot to mention. Mortimer visited me while I was working in the rose garden."

"What did he want?"

"He was heading into the village and invited me to join him. I told him I had other plans."

He said nothing, as though searching for the right words. "Interesting. Anything else?"

She told him of her uneasiness being around him and what he'd mentioned to her about his own family. "I thought you'd want to know. I was hoping it might help."

"Yes, it'll be quite helpful. I wrote Parr and told him about the man just showing up, so he'll send men around to investigate."

"Now they can investigate the village where he says he grew up. I thought his property was in the north."

"I intend to do just that. Anyway, I expect Parr to arrive soon. As far as his property, it is in the north, but there is an old family home nearby."

She smiled. "That explains a great deal. Your sister will arrive soon as well."

"Yes, and you'll like Frannie."

He ran his thumb slowly across her cheek. "Gabriel?"

"Hmmm?"

"What was it you said you wanted to discuss with me?"

His face turned even more serious that it had been. "Marry me, Savannah."

Her mind danced around that word—marry. It sent a thousand different thoughts racing through her mind. Did she dare marry this man? Though she already cared for him deeply, love was another matter.

"Gabriel, what brings this on? We haven't known each other two months, and you propose marriage?"

"Others marry in mere weeks. Love is something that grows with time."

"You still haven't answered my question: what brings this on?"

"I find myself falling in love with you, and now just seems to be a perfect time," he replied. He brushed her cheek.

She sighed at his touch. "It wouldn't have anything to do with everything going on with Lady Dorset, would it?"

"No, though I will admit I'm uneasy with both Lady Dorset and Mortimer."

She gazed into his eyes. "You could just offer us your protection if you feel that strongly."

"It's not the same. I want more. I want you."

She kissed his finger as he ran it across her lips. "Will you give me time to think about it? I only ask because I have Vincent to take into account."

He appeared disappointed, but regardless of her own feelings, she had to take her son into consideration. This was a huge commitment, and Gabriel had been the last man she would have thought would propose marriage. They'd had a tumultuous relationship starting out. Could they make it work? The last thing she wanted to have happen was to find herself in a loveless marriage, with her and her husband leading separate lives and Gabriel coming to her bedchambers only to use her body for his needs. No, that wasn't how she envisioned marriage. This time around, she was wiser, and she knew what was involved, what she wanted.

"Since the subject makes you ill at ease at the moment, we'll discuss it another time."

She nodded. "Your proposal doesn't make me feel ill at ease. There is more to it than just my saying yes."

"Understood. Just don't play with my feelings, Savannah."

"I could never do that to you, nor would I."

Slowly, with both hands on her face he drew her toward him. He leaned down and caught her lips with his. Her hand curled around his nape, running her fingers through his hair while the other drifted up to his chest. She shivered as he nibbled at an earlobe, making her shiver.

"Gabriel, someone might enter."

"Anyone opening that door without announcing themselves knows they'll be let go," he replied.

"I'm not used to this."

"What? Being with a man outside the bedroom? What about the tower?"

"That was different."

"Should I lock the door? Or should I take you to my chambers using a secret passageway?"

"A secret passageway?"

He nodded. "Yes. Most old castles had them. They were mainly used to hide women and children during a siege or to escape the castle undetected."

"And your valet?"

"Knows if the door to my chamber is closed not to disturb me," he growled. He rose from the settee and headed across the room.

"Where are you going?"

"To lock the door. I'm going to make love to you."

He dropped to his knees in front of her and lifted her skirts. Quickly removing her undergarments and parting her legs, he gazed down at her. Her breath hitched in anticipation of what came next. He ran his fingers over her hipbones before running his tongue along her folds.

She moaned low as his tongue pressed against her clitoris before sucking and making her quiver with anticipation. He lifted her legs and raised them over his shoulders and continued to tease her with his tongue. Finally, all the buildup exploded, taking her over the edge. He lifted his head and mounted her, grinding his hardened cock against her wet womanhood.

Hurriedly, she fumbled at the placard of his breeches to open them and spring his cock free of its prison.

She reached for his cock and found the tip wet. She smeared the wetness onto her thigh, then guided him to her opening. Another small orgasm raced through her as he penetrated her. He pushed farther.

"Don't stop," she whispered.

He continued deeper into her and pushed until he was seated to the hilt. He began to slowly thrust in and out as they established a rhythm together.

"You feel so good," he gasped.

"Gabriel!" She cried out his name as she met him stroke for stroke.

Finally, he exploded inside her. Her name and other filthy words flew from his mouth as he finally slowed and pushed one last time. They remained like that for a few moments. He didn't know if it were mere seconds, a minute, an hour, or a day. He was in utopia and never wanted it to end. He wanted to carry her upstairs and take her again, this time completely naked, where he could taste her breasts and feel the rest of her body against his.

"I want more," he murmured. "I want to touch every part of your body. I want you to touch me."

"I do too."

"You do?" He hadn't expected that from her.

"Yes. Is the tower far from here?"

"Far enough, but it sounds like rain is hitting the windows."

"Drat," she replied. "I suppose we're left with no choice but to stay in your chambers, Your Grace."

He laughed and kissed her. "Get dressed."

They put themselves to right and then left the library and stepped into the hallway. It was eerily quiet, but then Gabriel's servants knew how to disappear into the woodwork. Taking her hand, he led her into a small dining room.

"What is this?" she asked, eyeing the table laid out with food.

"I thought we'd enjoy lunch in here. I was going to have it served on the balcony, but the weather changed all that."

"This is nice. Is it where you usually take your meals?"

He nodded. "Yes. The main dining room is far too big for one or two people. I started out having breakfast here, and it grew into eating all my meals here."

"I like it. I wish Lady Dorset would allow us to take other meals in the breakfast room, but as you saw, she's quite consumed by tradition."

"As I told you, it's your decision to make, not Lady Dorset's. Hopefully, she'll move into the dower house in a few days. It'll make it easier for you to make such decisions," he said with a smirk. "Of course, you could always marry me and move here, where you'd be my duchess and in charge of the household."

"Gabriel…"

"I know, I know. You wish a few days."

She speared a strawberry from her plate. "I'm afraid you're going to have to have your carriage take me back if this rain doesn't let up. I hope it clears up, or else everyone's going to know where I've been."

"And that matters to you? It shouldn't."

"I know it shouldn't matter, but I have Vincent to think of."

"As you've reminded me several times," he replied gruffly.

He was letting his frustration show. He didn't mean anything by it. As much as she really wanted to marry him, she needed to discuss it with Vincent. Ever since Roland had died, the one thing Savannah had been was honest and forthcoming.

"I'll give you my answer in a couple of days."

"About what?" he inquired slyly.

"You know very well to what I refer."

Before Gabriel could answer, there was a knock on the door. The butler, Simmons, apologized for interrupting their meal and walked across the room to Gabriel to present him with a silver tray containing correspondence. Gabriel nodded and took the paper.

"The man is waiting for a reply, Your Grace."

Gabriel nodded as he broke the seal. "Send him to the kitchen to eat. Tell him I'll have my reply shortly."

After the door closed behind the butler, Gabriel sat back in his chair and read the message. Savannah tried not to stare but couldn't help herself. She found she was fascinated trying to imagine what the message might be about just by the expressions on Gabriel's face.

"I hope everything is all right," she said. She picked up a piece of cheddar cheese and bit into it. It was made on Gabriel's estate and was among the best she'd tasted.

"This is from Parr. He'll be here in three days. In the meantime, he tells me our runner has found out that Mortimer does reside in India, but does not work for the Crown."

"Whom does he work for if not the Crown?"

"It seems he works for the East India Company. He procures spices and tea, along with salt."

"Why would he lie about what he does?"

"I imagine because part of his job is to purchase opium."

She shook her head. "Opium? That would explain it. Many people have mixed emotions about it."

"True," he replied. "Anyway, Parr states he'll give me a more detailed briefing once he arrives at Brook Fall."

She nodded. "You best write him a reply."

"I shall once we've finished eating. I thought you would enjoy a walk through the castle afterwards."

"Yes, I would. This is the only castle I've ever been in," she said, picking up another piece of cheese. "This cheese is quite delicious."

Gabriel smiled. "I'll make sure you get a wheel when you leave."

"Thank you."

"It is made here on my estate, and enough is made to sell to a shop in the village as well as a couple of other villages."

"What else do you make?"

"We smoke hams and sell them to some of the local butchers in the area."

"So the estate is making money to keep it running?"

He nodded, picking up a piece of cheese and bread. "Yes. As with most estates, the grains are grown to sell, cattle and sheep are raised for consumption. The rest of it are the fruits of labor."

"Does Vincent's estate do the same?"

"Yes, though when the dowager countess got me

involved, I found the estate had been losing money because some things were being neglected."

"I trust you've righted the situation?"

"Yes. By next year, it should start to turn around."

She nodded. "That's good to know. I'm grateful for all you've done."

"No need." He speared a strawberry and popped it into his mouth. Gabriel rose. "If you'll excuse me for a few minutes, I'm going to go write Parr a reply."

"Go ahead. I think I'll sit here and enjoy a cup of tea."

"Don't forget to try the pineapple. It's grown in a greenhouse here on the estate."

"You have a pineapple stove?"

"Yes," he replied as he moved toward the door.

"I want to see it." She watched as he walked through the opening and the door closed.

She was indeed grateful Gabriel was overseeing Vincent's interests. He had some grand ideas. She would make some notes this evening and talk with Gabriel in more detail about them. If he could do it, why couldn't they? Even if she accepted his marriage proposal, it would be nice to have Vincent's estate make extra money. By the time he would be old enough to take over the earldom, he would have a comfortable cushion with which to run his estate.

Her mind wandered to Mortimer. What did he want? He must be successful at what he did for the East India Company, but why just show up? It occurred to her that word probably hadn't reached him in India about the death of his two cousins. He most likely thought he was returning to England to take his place as earl, and instead found the title passed on to Vincent, who was the rightful heir. Until Vincent married and had children of his own, Mortimer would be her son's heir.

Was that why he'd returned? She needed to bring up the matter with Gabriel as soon as possible. He needed to know her thoughts. After all, the situation could be as simple as Mortimer presented. Still, something niggled at her.

CHAPTER 21

Savannah's mind had been made up. She would marry Gabriel. She had told him she would give his proposal some consideration, and after a couple of days decided she didn't need to look any further. Gabriel was a reformed rake, and those, she understood, made the best husbands. He'd certainly proven that already. He adored Vincent and would make sure her son would grow up to be a fine young man. In addition, Vincent worshiped Gabriel, mimicking him every chance he got, regardless if Gabriel was there or not.

She'd been invited to dine at the duke's castle this evening, and knowing Gabriel's friend Parr had arrived, she hoped she and Gabriel would have a moment alone in order that she might tell him her decision. The duke's carriage swayed from side to side as it now carried her to his castle.

Hopefully, Parr had some answers about her late husband's long-lost cousin, Mortimer Dawson. The only thing she knew before was what little Mortimer had told her and what Parr had found out on his own.

The dowager countess and Mortimer had both been invited to dine at the duke's this evening, but Lady

Dorset declined. Grudgingly, she'd moved into the dower house a couple of days before and seemed to realize that living there, she could have her own life— away from the past.

Mortimer, on the other hand, had declined the duke's invitation, stating a prior engagement with the village vicar, which Savannah found suspicious at best. She doubted the man had stepped inside a church in years. She had mentioned it to Gabriel when he'd come to visit Vincent the day before.

As the carriage pulled up in front of Gabriel's castle, she said a little prayer that the evening proved to be as perfect as she envisioned it would. The evening was cooler than most, a reminder that autumn was just around the corner.

A footman helped her descend from the carriage just as Gabriel walked through the door. "Good evening, Your Grace." He was the most gorgeous man she'd ever laid eyes on, and it wouldn't matter if he lived in a shack in the woods. She would still love him.

He smiled and took her hand. "Mrs. Dawson."

He led her through the front door, to the drawing room. A fire in the hearth beckoned them closer. She walked over and turned to face Gabriel, who watched her intently.

"Sherry?" he inquired.

She nodded. "Your friend Parr, did he arrive?"

"Yes, though he won't be joining us this evening. Fool decided to ride all the way from London. His horse threw a shoe, so he ended up walking the last few miles," he replied as he poured two glasses of sherry.

He crossed the room to pass her a glass, smiling the entire way. What was going through his mind?

"He must be exhausted."

"He is, but looks forward to seeing you while he's here."

"Has he got the answers you were seeking?" She asked taking a sip of sherry. She walked over to a dark blue settee and sat, placing the glass of sherry on a table in front of her.

"He says he does, but we'll speak in the morning."

"I see. That means it's just you and me this evening."

He arched a brow and smiled. "Yes."

"It seems a pity to use that huge dining room if there's only the two of us. Could you have them serve dinner in the smaller room?"

He took a sip of sherry and nodded. "I took the liberty to have dinner taken up to my personal sitting room."

Personal sitting room meant the one in his chambers. The one he shared with no one. "You must have been sure I'd agree to dining with you in your private chambers."

He smiled seductively. "I did it on the hunch we'd be spending the evening discussing private matters," he said. He reached over and took her hand. "You said you had something you wished to discuss with me."

"Yes, I do."

After a knock on the door, the butler entered. "Dinner is ready, Your Grace."

"Thank you, Higgins. I can handle the rest. I'll set the dishes in the hall when we're finished."

She wondered if he was telling the butler they weren't to be disturbed without saying the words. She was entering his inner sanctum, and not everyone was allowed there.

He turned to her. "Shall we?"

She finished her glass of sherry and set the glass back on the table. "Yes."

He led her upstairs and down a hall to two massive oak doors. The duke's chambers. A footman opened a door, and Savannah entered as she heard

Gabriel say something to the footman before the door was closed.

She marveled at the heavy dark furniture. It was terribly masculine. She wondered how long it had been here. Near a long window sat a table set for two. Nearby, a brass serving cart stood with two bottles of wine, dessert, and an assortment of cheese and fruit.

He neared and helped her into one of the two chairs. He removed the lids from their plates before sitting across from her.

Roasted pheasant along with roasted potatoes and vegetables were neatly arranged on the plate. A basket of bread sat to one side. She watched as he picked up the bottle of wine and poured them both a glass.

"This is quite pleasant," she casually remarked. She found herself nervous, her hands trembling ever so slightly. Never before had she been in a chamber so elegant, and certainly not one belonging to a duke.

"I sometimes like to eat here if it's just myself. Especially on a rainy evening. The castle is drafty, but it's small enough in here, the drafts don't seem to bother."

"How long has your family lived here?"

"I'm the twelfth duke, so we've lived here since the first duke was gifted the castle and surrounding lands. That makes me the twelfth generation to live in the castle."

"That's a long time. I could never imagine."

"Everything is new in America, no?"

"Yes, for the most part," she replied. She took a bite of the pheasant. I was delicious and could melt in her mouth.

"Do you miss it?" he asked as he watched her intently.

"Surprisingly not as much as I thought I would. Certainly, I miss certain aspects of it—my parents and family, friends, but not as much as I anticipated."

Finally, Gabriel cleared their plates and set the cheese and fruit in the center of the table. He poured her another glass of wine before sitting down. She was nervous, unsure how to broach the subject of marriage with him. She decided to act coy and see how he responded. Knowing Gabriel, he'd pick right up on what she intended to say.

"Didn't you ask something?"

He nodded. "Yes, and you wanted to think it through."

"I can't recall what it was you asked," she teased.

He leaned back in his chair, picked up his glass of wine, and smiled. He swirled the liquid before responding. "I believe I asked you to marry me."

"And I have my answer, Gabriel."

"Go on."

"Yes. Yes, I'll marry you."

Setting the glass down on the table, he rose and made his way next to her, taking both her hands in his. "Truly?"

"Yes."

He leaned in and kissed her—gently at first. The kiss deepened before it ended, and he smiled. "You've made me a very happy man, Savannah. What changed your mind?"

"My mind didn't need to be changed. I knew I would agree to marry you. I just needed to take some time for myself. It is a huge decision and one I didn't take lightly."

He sat again and swallowed his wine. "When would you like to marry?"

He was asking her. Not even Roland had done that. He'd simply arranged the entire matter.

"As soon as we can arrange it. Something small and private. Unless, of course, you wish something larger."

"Small and private is perfect. I'll arrange for a special license if that suits you."

"That is fine," she replied. "There's much to be decided and done before then. I don't have much, Gabriel. Roland left me little, as you know his shipping interests are now Vincent's."

"Since Vincent is an earl and has everything an earldom has to offer, how about we put anything extra in an account for any daughters we might have?"

"You're sure?"

"I would rather do that than keep it."

His thoughtfulness brought her close to tears. She wiped them away. "Thank you, Gabriel."

"Come, there is no need for tears. This is a happy occasion, is it not?"

"Yes. Very happy."

Then he drew in a deep breath and let it out slowly. "There is one other thing I must tell you, Savannah."

She felt her heart stutter as the joy faded from his eyes.

"Years ago," he said, "I was engaged to be married. I thought I loved Marie, and she me. But on the day we were to be wed, she eloped with another man."

Savannah shook her head. "How terrible for you."

He nodded. "At the time, it was devastating. I vowed I'd never fall in love again, let alone marry. But now…I find I want to spend my life with you, to give you everything I have. To have children of our own, if you would like. You have made me believe in love again."

"As you have me, Gabriel." She reached across the table to cover his hand with hers.

He turned his hand over and gripped her fingers, then gave her the lopsided grin she adored. "While we are here, would you care to see the duchess's chambers?"

"That's not necessary. We can do it another day."

"Really, it's not a bother. There's a door over there that leads into the duchess's sitting room."

She'd forgotten the aristocracy partook in such practices. She stood and gazed at him. "Then show me."

He circled the table to join her. "The rooms haven't been used since my mother occupied them. Feel free to redecorate as you wish."

Picking up a candle and taking her hand, he led her to the door that separated a husband and wife. Fortunately, the moon was at half and shone through the window. From best she could tell, the room was done in white, with furniture she believed came from France. Very ornate. The entire suite of rooms was quite feminine—from another era.

"I'd like to see it in the daylight."

"Of course. I want you to make it your own, though I do have one request."

She nodded as she strolled through the rooms. The wall covering seemed faded from time. He was right; it all needed to be redone.

"What is that?"

"I would hope you would sleep with me in my chambers, using yours to bathe and dress."

"Of course. I'd like that. Very much."

Setting the candle down on a table, he gathered her in his arms. "You've made me very happy, Savannah. I hope you'll be happy here."

Before she could reply, he kissed her. This time, the kiss was one of passion, of making his intentions known. She opened to him, her arms around his neck and her fingers intertwined in his dark-blond hair.

He ended the kiss with a hungry look. "You belong to me, and I intend to show you," he growled with implacable confidence. He kissed her again, this time his hands pulled her next to his firm body. As he brought her closer, she caught the fragrance of his shaving soap and the man. She was so caught up in him and the moment that she almost didn't realize anything else existed.

"Come. I will show you the rooms tomorrow in the daylight," he said. He picked up the candle and led her back into his suite of rooms.

"Where is the nursery?" she asked.

"It's easier to show you rather than explain, but I will tell you this. It is on this floor, but beyond a door that separates the nursery from this area of the house. There is another set of stairs to access it."

"I take it you and your siblings spent a lot of time there?"

"Yes, of course. My mother, though, did make a point of visiting with us once or twice a day. She would come have tea with us, and she always came in to say good night. As I hope to say good night to you, with a kiss, every night from here to forever."

His mouth covered hers, and he kissed her deeply, his tongue slipping past her lips to toy with hers. He tasted like liquor and perhaps cigars. She felt his fingers working her clothing until she was down to her chemise. Slowly, he pulled it over her head. His hands reached for her breasts, stroking them tenderly before he pinched her nipple. He led her to the bed and quickly undressed before kissing her neck.

"Gabriel," she moaned.

She ran her hands down his back. He was nude, his skin hot to the touch. He lay atop her, his weight settling between her thighs.

She felt the tip of his cock nudge her as he found her entrance and thrust inside. He shifted back and rocked, gently, each small thrust pushing him deeper. He hooked his hands under her knees and lifted them over his shoulders. He kissed her mouth, then feathered kisses to her breasts, torturing her.

He was in control, and would make love to her in the manner he desired. She arched up, silently asking him to touch her more. She ran her hands through his hair and hung on, kissing him back and moving submissively under him.

He groaned as his hips worked a little faster, his cock deep inside her. She felt each thrust and moaned, wanting more. She arched her back and met him with equal fervor. She wanted this man more than life itself.

He broke their kiss and slid his fingers down her side, between their bodies. He pressed his thumb down on her clitoris.

"Come with me," he rasped. His shoulders were bunched with muscle, strands of hair clinging to his face as his green eyes stared wildly into hers.

"I can't."

His thumb circled her nipple as his cock continued to fill her.

She arched her head and cried out, his mouth catching the sound. She'd never experienced anything like this before. He propped himself up on his elbows and kissed her gently as he made love to her, then threw back his head as his body jerked into hers. He called out her name as his seed flooded her.

"My God, Savannah, what are you doing to me?"

Slowly, he withdrew and lay on his side, pulling her close to him. Savannah had never felt such bliss before. She absentmindedly ran her fingers through his chest hair, feeling his chest rise and fall as he settled.

"I could ask the same thing of you."

"What?"

She sat up. "I've never experienced the closeness I feel when we're one."

He smiled. "Good to know. There is so much more I want to teach you. That is, if you're interested."

"Yes. I want you to show me."

He grinned. "I can't wait until we're married and don't have to sneak around."

"We're not sneaking around, Gabriel. You have a houseful of servants who know exactly what we're about."

"Which is none of their concern," he replied briskly. He got out of bed. "Brandy?"

"Yes, please."

Someone knocked quite hard on the outside door. Gabriel threw on his banyan and stormed out of the room. "The castle better be on fire, or else I intend to sack whoever's on the other side of that door."

She couldn't understand what was being said as the door to his chamber was closed. All she could hear were raised voices at first. Then the door shut, and the chamber door flew open. Gabriel's scowl told her something was terribly amiss.

He sat beside her on the bed and took one of her hands. "That was Higgins. Seems your butler dispatched a footman to come."

"Why? Is Vincent ill?"

He shook his head. "No."

"What's the problem? Higgins wouldn't send someone if it weren't important. Tell me what it is, Gabriel."

"Vincent seems to be missing."

"Missing? Impossible. They should know him well enough to know he loves to explore at any hour of the day or night."

"True, but he's nowhere to be found," he replied softly. "Mortimer is nowhere to be found either. They're both gone."

She gasped and clutched her chest. "Are you saying Mortimer took Vincent?"

"I don't know yet."

"We have to go. We must find him."

"The carriage is being readied. Let's dress, and we'll go to Sky View. I'll wake Parr. He might be able to help. He's good at this sort of thing."

She began to pick up her clothes from the floor and dressed. "Has Lady Dorset been informed? He could be there, at the dower house."

"Right now, I'm not sure. If she hasn't been, I'll send someone to tell her."

A few minutes later, she was ready. She pinned her hair back up as neatly as she could, her fingers trembling as she did. Her body shook with fear. Fear of the unknown and what had happened to her son. She rushed downstairs and found Gabriel and another man in the drawing room talking.

"Mrs. Dawson, may I present the Earl of Wexford," Gabriel said when he noticed her.

"Mrs. Dawson," the earl greeted her. "Please call me Parr. All my friends do."

She nodded and asked Gabriel, "Have you told him what's going on and about Mortimer?"

"We were just discussing the matter. After we speak with Higgins, we'll know better which way to take the search."

"Why would he take Vincent?"

Parr cleared his throat. "I'm sure it has something to do with the earldom. Have you heard him mention that or his feeling cheated when he found out Vincent had taken his rightful place?"

"No. All I know is what he told us about living in India."

A footman opened the drawing room door and stepped inside.

"Come, the carriage awaits," Gabriel said.

She walked alongside Gabriel, and Parr followed. No one said a word, but Savannah was grateful she had these two strong men with her. On her own, she might not fare so well.

~

SKY VIEW WAS LIT up with torches when they arrived. Savannah descended from the carriage and rushed to the house before Gabriel could even help her down. Inside, they were met by a distraught Higgins, who took the young earl's disappearance personally.

"Higgins, it's not your fault," Savannah told the butler.

Gabriel interrupted. "I've sent Parr to talk with the footmen who were on the grounds at the time of Vincent's disappearance. They'll tell us where they've already searched for the boy." He turned to Higgins. "Have the stables been checked?"

"Yes, Your Grace, and the greenhouse as well. The maids have checked every room in the house, as well as the basement. If he's here, he's hiding well."

"Did anyone see Dawson this evening?"

"He went to the village to eat. Told Cook not to go to all the fuss of preparing dinner for one."

"And he never returned?" Savannah asked.

"No, madam."

"Has anyone told Lady Dorset?"

"No, madam. No one wished to wake her until you were informed." Higgins was stoic as always, ready to do whatever was asked of him.

Savannah nodded, then lifted her skirts and turned toward the door.

"Where are you going?" Gabriel asked.

"To wake the dowager countess, of course."

CHAPTER 22

*I*t didn't surprise Gabriel at all that Savannah took matters into her own hands. She stayed on top of everything that was going on as they searched for young Vincent. Certainly, she was worried, but he knew her well enough to recognize this was all a cover to keep her emotions in check so she didn't break down.

Parr returned, finding no sign of either Vincent or Mortimer. Gabriel began to wonder if they were even in the area. They would have been able to put considerable distance between them if the man had planned this in the first place. Parr thought the same thing and suggested they send for the local authorities. It was clear as day this was a kidnapping.

As dawn began to break and weary searchers returned to Sky View empty-handed, Savannah made sure everyone was fed and plenty of coffee and tea made available. She appeared tired, dark circles beneath her eyes as she pushed a serving cart containing tea into his study. No English lady would have taken on the difficult task, but would have left the work to servants. His heart swelled with pride that his future duchess was not afraid to do what needed to be done.

"Lady Dorset? How was she?" he asked as he accepted a cup from her.

"Hysterical, of course. I wouldn't expect her to react any other way. She offered to send some men to assist."

"Good. The more hands, the better," Gabriel replied.

She passed a cup to Parr, who'd been sitting quietly in a worn leather chair in front of the fire. "I suggested she have her staff go through her house."

"I imagine she was mortified by that," Gabriel said quietly.

"Actually, no."

"It's probably best you woke her to tell her. Knowing the countess, I'm sure she would have been quite indignant if she found out a search had been going on while she slept."

Savannah sighed. "What do you suggest we do now? Expand our search?"

"Yes. I've sent a man to fetch the authorities. We'll widen the search once they arrive."

"Good," she replied.

Gabriel could see she was far more than fatigued and led her to the other chair by the fire. "Here, sit for a few minutes."

"But if there's news or someone needs me…" she protested.

"They'll know where to find you."

"What does Mortimer think he's going to gain by all this? If it's money he wants…"

"It may well be," Parr said. "I believe he thought you'd never leave America. That way, he could claim the earldom. You thwarted his plans when you and Vincent arrived."

"You're right," she said softly.

"All we have to do is find out where he's taken Vincent," Parr said.

"They could be anywhere."

"He owns nothing, and as far as Parr's been able to find out, Mortimer lives in London," Gabriel said.

"If that's where he's taken Vincent, it could take weeks to find them. London's a huge place, and hiding would not be a problem if you knew where to go," Parr said.

"Then send men to London to search for him. You've got runners working. Use them to flush him out."

"I'm sending word to my man, explaining the situation and to expand the search," Parr replied.

She rose from her chair. "I can't just sit here and do nothing. Vincent is out there with a strange man, who knows where. We must find them."

"And we will. They've got at least a couple of hours' start on us, and we have no idea where Mortimer would have taken him."

"Are we overlooking any cottages or buildings on the estate? What about Brook Fall? Is there anywhere he could hide there?"

"There is the tower, but that's in plain sight," Gabriel replied. "Now that it's daylight, we can have the men go through all the empty cottages."

"He's not here," Parr said grimly. "He wouldn't be so brazen as to keep him so close."

Gabriel arched a brow. "Where, then?"

"I suggest expanding the search to nearby villages. He's going to want to stay close to follow what's going on here."

"I don't know what he expects to gain except money."

The two men looked at each other but said nothing in front of Savannah. He and Parr already knew the man probably wanted what he saw as rightfully his: the earldom. With Vincent out of the way, he could come back to claim it. How long he would remain hidden to do this was undetermined. Gabriel figured him for a greedy man. He'd make a mistake, which was why it was imperative they find the pair soon. The longer it took, the more likely Vincent's life hung in the balance.

"Why don't you go lie down for a while? I'll come get you the moment the constable arrives."

"I wouldn't be able to sleep, but I believe I'll retire upstairs and change."

Both men stood as Savannah walked across the room and out of sight. Gabriel knew she knew the seriousness of the situation, and why her son was probably taken. She was smart and observant of her surroundings.

"Is there anywhere else we should be looking?" Gabriel asked as he sat next to Parr.

"Not at the moment. As far as we know, he owns no property," Parr remarked.

"He wouldn't chance taking Vincent there if he did. He'll keep him somewhere close, like you said. Perhaps he found a cottage to let," Gabriel added.

"Or found an old abandoned one," Parr said.

Gabriel tapped his fingers on the chair arms. "I think we need to check my estate a little closer. There are some old abandoned cottages on the southeast corner. They aren't in particularly good shape, but would do for a day or two."

"Shall I send out a party to search the area?"

"Yes, make sure someone from my estate is present. They'll know where to look."

As Parr was about to take his leave, Higgins knocked and brought in a message. "This came for Mrs. Dawson, but I was told she is lying down. I thought you should read it."

He passed the paper to Gabriel and began to leave, but Gabriel stopped the butler. "Wait."

He scanned the paper and reread to make sure his eyes hadn't deceived him the first time.

"Is it from Dawson?"

Gabriel nodded. "Yes. It seems he wants the ten thousand pounds in exchange for Vincent."

"We were right. He wants money. He says it's his due for what Roland did to him."

"I see." He turned to Higgins. "Who brought this, and are they still here?"

"Yes, a boy brought it. Told me a man who fit Lord Dawson's description instructed him to bring it to the house in exchange for some coin."

"Do you recognize the lad?" Gabriel asked.

"No, Your Grace."

"Very well. See he is fed while I'll come talk to the boy shortly. Perhaps he'll tell me something, like where he picked up the note.'"

The butler disappeared, and Gabriel turned to his friend. "This means he isn't far. He'd never send a boy if he weren't nearby."

"I agree. Vincent will slow him down, not to mention he's going to figure everyone is looking for him. How do you want to play this?"

He knew Savannah was going to be angry with him for making decisions without consulting her, but she needed her rest if she was to be any assistance in finding her son.

"I'm going to acknowledge him and tell him that amount of money simply isn't lying around. That it'll take some time to procure it."

"Ask him how Vincent is."

"I planned to."

"I'll send a runner to follow the boy."

"Good idea, but make sure it's someone who will blend in in case Mortimer sees him. I don't want him spooked."

Gabriel hurried and penned his reply. He hoped this would buy them enough time in their search. Mortimer was by no means stupid, but the man also didn't seem to have a real grasp of the world. He thought if he wished it, it would happen. The longer he thought the money was his, the longer he'd treat Vincent with care.

"Go find your man. I'm going to the kitchens to give this to the boy and size him up. I'll lead him out the kitchen door."

"I'll have him close by."

"I hope this works," Gabriel muttered. "I hate when children are involved."

"As do I."

The two men walked to the grand hall, and Gabriel headed down a back hall toward the kitchens while Parr went in search of the runner.

When Gabriel entered the kitchen, the maids stopped whatever task they were doing. It was highly irregular that a duke come to a kitchen. He ignored them, though he acknowledged the cook, who asked him if she could get him anything. He shook his head and walked toward the boy seated at the well-worn kitchen table. The room was redolent with smells that reminded Gabriel of being a boy and sneaking down to the kitchens at his own home.

"Here is my letter. Where are you to meet the gentleman who paid you?"

"I'm not. I'm to leave it in a special spot. He said too many like you would want to talk to him if we met."

Gabriel silently cursed. This wasn't what he intended. He should have known Dawson would take extra precautions. He'd make sure the runner stuck around and waited for the letter to be picked up.

"Very well." He reached into his waistcoat and pulled out a couple of coins. He placed them in the boy's hand. "This is for you."

"Thank you, sir, er, Your Grace."

Gabriel cocked his head. The boy was observant. He had been paying attention to what was going on around him, or else he wouldn't have heard the cook refer to him by his title.

He turned on his heel and left the kitchen. Though he could use a couple of hours' sleep, Gabriel refused to allow himself the luxury. He owed it to Savannah to see that her son was returned safely. He wouldn't rest until young Vincent was reunited with his mother.

Love. That's what this must be. It was still hard for him to conceive that he actually loved a woman for who she was and what she thought. He'd resisted long enough, and now he couldn't wait to make her his wife. She already was his in other ways. There was no reason to put things off. As soon as he could make the arrangements and get the license, they would marry.

He would be better prepared to see to her and Vincent's safety once they were living at Brook Fall. Nothing could have prevented this turn of events. Dawson had planned this and would have waited until the time was right. They'd left Vincent in capable hands, and Dawson had preyed on that. They'd made it too easy for him.

~

SAVANNAH AWOKE WITH A START. She'd only meant to come upstairs to change, where she undressed from the gown she'd been wearing since the night before. She had no intention to be gone but a short time. Instead, she'd made the mistake of lying down and falling asleep. She wondered how long she'd slept.

Her maid appeared out of nowhere. "I took the liberty to draw a bath, madam. I thought perhaps you'd like to bathe and freshen up before rejoining the duke and his friend."

"Thank you."

She padded into the bathing chamber, removed the remainder of her clothing, and climbed into the tub of warm water. As she did, she picked up Gabriel's musky scent from their lovemaking the night before. While she desperately tried to convince herself it wasn't her fault for her son's abduction, she wondered. Had she stayed at home, would Mortimer have taken Vincent, or had this been spur of the moment? She refused to blame herself. If this had been the man's intention all along, nothing could have prevented the events of last night from happening.

Vincent would be found because Mortimer wasn't that smart, nor did he have the means to keep them in hiding. What would happen if he ran out of funds or simply grew tired of the fact she wasn't going to give in to his demands? Surely, he wouldn't harm her son.

After dressing, she rejoined Gabriel and Parr, who were standing in the drawing room talking with a man not too much older than Gabriel. He was nodding, and the man who accompanied him was furiously taking notes at a nearby desk. She deducted this man must be the constable.

Introductions were made, then the constable, Tommy Burns, asked Savannah a few questions. Where might Vincent go, who did he know... Certainly, Gabriel must have told him, so the man was asking the wrong set of questions. What concerned her the most was that her young son had been fairly well sheltered since arriving. Most of his contact had been with the people who lived on the estate, and even that had been limited thanks to Lady Dorset.

"If that is all, I'm going to check on Lady Dorset."

She paused and turned to Gabriel. "I'll need a carriage or even a wagon when I return."

"Of course. Where are you planning on going?" he asked.

"To Brook Fall. I thought to make sure everyone who is helping out should be fed. If we split the cooking duties, we'll stop driving both our cooks mad."

He smiled. "An excellent idea," he replied. "Let me walk you to the door."

She said her goodbyes to the constable and Parr before quitting the room with Gabriel right behind her.

"I take it nothing has changed?" she asked.

"No, but these things can take time," he replied.

"Very well. I'm going to try to talk the dowager countess into rising and coming to oversee making sure everyone has a hot meal as they return. I'll do the same at Brook Fall."

He arched a brow and placed his hand on her waist. "I'll have the carriage readied. I think you'll find my cook quite well organized."

"I'm sure I will, but I merely thought to take some of the burden off her. I think both households working together is important right now. Besides, it keeps my mind occupied."

"I'll send word if anything changes."

"Please do, because I got the distinct feeling the constable is one of those men who thinks things like this should be taken care of by the men, and the women need to be sheltered from all of it."

"You may be right. I best return to them so we can put together a plan. If Mortimer feels Roland swindled him, he won't give up Vincent until he gets what he feels he's owed."

She paused. "What does that mean? What Roland owes him? Roland never even mentioned him."

His eyes grew even more serious. 'Savannah, I didn't

want to say more until my research was complete, but I have reason to suspect your husband may have been involved in something illegal. Before he died he took out a substantial loan, and several of his ships mysteriously disappeared. The man I sent to research the situation has informed me Roland may have been involved in the opium trade, and his ships were sunk by a rival. In fact, that might account for his death as well."

Her hand flew to her chest. "And where does Mortimer fit in?"

He arched a brow. "I suspect he invested in Roland's scheme. When Roland died at sea, Mortimer would have lost everything. This is likely why he is demanding ransom now. It's the only thing that makes sense."

"Of course." She stood on tiptoe and kissed his cheek. "Thank you for sharing all this," she said, adding, "I will check on the dowager. Perhaps she has more information about Mortimer that will help in the search."

Savannah walked to the dower house, struggling to reconcile the Roland she knew with the blackguard Gabriel described. It was true Roland's business had consumed his life and taken him away from her and Vincent. As much as she didn't want to admit it, Gabriel's assessment rang true. Now there was nothing left to do but defeat Mortimer and rescue her son.

At least they had help now. The constable seemed to know the people of this area quite well, and he knew the terrain like the back of his hand. He mentioned to her he'd lived there all his life, so no one would be able to hide for long. He would find them, probably in some long-abandoned cottage or barn. Not the best scenario when she pictured her son right now, but it was better than them being out in the elements.

She wondered how Vincent was faring. Was he scared, was he cold, was he getting fed? Thankfully,

Roland had taken him on hunting trips a few times and had begun to teach Vincent how to survive in the wilderness, something she always thought him too young for, but Roland had convinced her a boy was never too young to learn survival skills. They would be invaluable to him should he ever need them in the future. She hoped he remembered what his father taught him now.

She found Lady Dorset seated in comfortable floral print chair staring out the window of her sitting room. Having never seen the dowager countess in this state, Savannah was pleasantly surprised by what she found: Lady Dorset having a cup of tea. She wasn't dressed, but wore a cream-colored dressing gown. She saw Savannah and began to get up. Savannah shook her head.

"Please, stay seated. No reason to get up."

"Is there any word about my grandson?"

She shook her head. "No, not yet, but I feel confident this constable will find him soon."

"Tommy Burns? Yes, I understand he's one of the best. London tried to recruit him. If anyone can find Vincent, it'll be Tommy."

"That's good to know."

"Now, is there anything I can do to help?" Lady Dorset asked as she set her tea down on the white table next to her. Everything seemed to be done in the white French provincial style that was all the rave in some circles.

"I wasn't expecting you to be out of bed, but now that you are, yes. I was going to ask you to go to Sky View and make sure there's enough food and drink for all the searchers. I know it may overwhelm Cook."

"It will. Cooking is her world. Don't worry, I'll take care of the rest."

"Thank you. I plan to go to Brook Fall and do the

same. There is much going on, and the staff are going to be stretched thin."

"Fortunately, there are well-organized housekeepers to assist."

"I thought it would help for us to be involved as well," Savannah added.

"I couldn't agree more. Give me about an hour to ready myself. If you wish, go on to Brook Fall. I can handle everything here."

"Thank you, Lady Dorset."

CHAPTER 23

wo more days had come and gone with still no sign of either Dawson or Vincent. Everyone was on edge. Savannah did her best to keep a brave face, when underneath, he knew she was beginning to be anxious. Each day that passed gave her more cause for her to worry.

The constable had sent word to the small village nearest Mortimer's home. He wanted to find out what sort of man Dawson was, who knew him, what his habits were. Anything to know the man better, and to figure out why he needed to obtain funds using such drastic measures.

While they waited for word from the north, the search continued. By now, the search had expanded, trying to take into consideration Dawson might use the dark of night to travel if he felt the need to leave the immediate area.

Gabriel didn't think he would risk taking Vincent too far, but at the same time, he might feel comfortable enough to take Vincent somewhere familiar to him, to his home, or close by. He knew Mortimer was smart enough to understand his home would be the first place authorities would search.

"You look like hell," Parr told him the third morning.

His friend was probably right. He'd barely slept, but knew if he did lie down, he'd sleep far too long. He ate only when reminded.

"Thanks for the update," he replied sarcastically.

"Why don't you go home for a while? Lie down, bathe, shave, eat. You need to have your wits about you."

"Thank you for your concern. My valet is here. He brought me what is necessary."

"You need to listen to your friend, Gabriel," Savannah said. "Your things are upstairs in the earl's bedchamber. Go. Take a bath, change, and lie down. When you're finished, I'll have Cook fix us a proper dinner."

Seeing he was outnumbered, Gabriel relented. "I'll do it. However, I do it with one request."

"What's that?" she asked.

"You wake me immediately should anything happen or change," he replied as he took Savannah's hand. "You, my dear, need to do the same."

"I already bathed and changed this morning. I slept, even if it was only for a couple of hours. It's you we're concerned about."

He sighed and, seeing he was outnumbered, retreated from the room. He beckoned Savannah to walk with him. She looked much better than he did. Her moss-green muslin day dress caught his eye. It was a color that suited her.

"Join me? You could help me wash," he said.

"Yes, and if I do, it'll turn into something else. I can't, Gabriel. I need to stay focused. When all this is over and Vincent is safely returned…"

"I plan on obtaining a special license, and we'll marry quickly. I'll not have you or Vincent living anywhere but under my roof."

"Very well. Agreed."

When they reached the bottom of the staircase, he took her in an embrace. "I've missed this," he whispered.

"As have I. Very much so, but you must go. Have Burns find me when you've awakened."

"I will, though I'd rather you come with me."

"Gabriel, go."

He kissed her lightly on the lips and she watched him as he headed up the stairs. She returned to where Parr stood looking out a window, hands in his pockets. He turned in her direction. "You know you're good for him."

"How do you mean?"

"He's not as restless. You've given him purpose."

"I can't take credit for that. He's maturing with life's situations."

"Do you know he's even talking about taking his seat in Parliament?"

She shook her head. "No, but then we haven't had much time to speak privately."

"He dotes on your son and loves you in ways I never imagined he could."

Smiling she sat before the hearth, where a fire blazed. The seasons were beginning to change, but to-day, rain seemed likely, making the air cooler. "Has he told you I was quite leery of him when we first arrived. I wasn't sure what to make of him."

"I was surprised when he told me that he'd agreed to mentor your son. It's so out of character for him."

"And now?"

"Now, I simply sit back in awe of him, and wonder if this is the same man I grew up with."

"Vincent adores him, and I, well, I find I've fallen madly in love with him as well."

He nodded and smiled in her direction. "I know."

"I'm not sure if Gabriel's ever shared much about my background, but marriage was the least of my priorities. Vincent is my world, and making sure he was educated to take over the earldom when he's older was my only concern."

"You're both doing an excellent job. I have no doubt young Vincent is going to make a fine earl."

"Thank you. I hope that holds true. I'm so afraid this incident will do harm."

"He'll be fine. This experience will, in the long run, make him stronger. Remember, children are resilient."

"Yes, they are."

Parr walked away from the window. "I believe I'll go check on things outside. It appears it's going to rain, and I saw a group of men headed back toward the house."

She nodded. "I look forward to our next conversation."

"As do I, Mrs. Dawson."

~

IT SUDDENLY OCCURRED to Gabriel as he lay in his tub that there was a portion of his estate he'd yet to send any search party to explore. Rocky and uninhabitable and surrounded by trees and thick forest growth, few knew it existed. No one tried to ride in such brutal terrain. Horses were known to slip, throwing their riders to the ground.

There was a small cave in the middle of the forest, sitting on a rise, hidden away. A brook ran not too far from the cave's entrance. He smiled. Actually, as a boy, he thought it to be a cave, when in reality, looking at it through adult eyes, it was no more than a place to hide out of the elements.

He remembered Timothy, Roland, and he used to go

there when they wanted to put a good scare in their respective governesses. Had Mortimer ever been with them? He couldn't recall because of Dawson's infrequent visits to Sky View. He and Timothy had been thick as thieves, always wandering off and leaving Roland and Gabriel to fend for themselves. Fortunately, his father had taught him survival skills since he was a young boy. His father always said there could come a time in one's life when they might find themselves alone and their very survival would depend on how well they knew how to live off the land.

Gabriel had brushed it off as his father living in a world gone by. He was a duke, and dukes never needed to have survival skills. They had people to cater to their every need.

His father, angry about his heir's noncompliant attitude, had ridden with his son late one afternoon and left him at the cave with no horse, no food, nothing. A storm swept in right as the old duke left, leaving Gabriel one of two choices. Wait it out until morning, or take the chance of being struck by lightning as he walked back to the castle. He'd chosen to stay. All through the night, he sat back as far as possible inside the small cave, scared at first. The more hours that passed, the less afraid Gabriel was. The next morning, he came out, tired, hungry, and thirsty and walked home. Never again did his father test him. He'd passed whatever test it was his father had been trying to put him through.

Survival.

After hurriedly dressing, Gabriel had a fresh horse brought around front. As he waited, he found Savannah speaking with the housekeeper. He was in awe how she put on a brave front, taking charge of everything rather than sitting down and waiting on others to do it for her.

He caught her eye as he walked across the room and nodded to the housekeeper. "I'm going to go look in an area we've neglected. The terrain is far too rough to ride, but there is somewhere that would be a perfect hiding place until things calmed down here."

"I would like to go with you, Your Grace," Savannah said.

He shook his head. "As I said, the terrain is unforgiving. I'll be back as soon as I can."

She gripped his arm, stopping him before he could leave. "I can't sit by while everyone else searches for my son. I'll go mad with worry if I'm not a part of the effort. If you love me, you must accept I'm not the kind of woman to let others do the work while I sit at home and wait. I *am* going with you."

He sighed, but recognized that she'd search for Vincent with him or without him. At least if they were together, she'd be safer. "Very well, my sweet."

As they walked together to the stables, then mounted their horses, he knew she wasn't happy, but he couldn't be angry with her. "Follow me," he instructed, then kicked his gelding into a gallop, and she raced along beside him without hesitation.

They rode hard until the land under them began to change, becoming rockier and more uneven. Gabriel put up his hand and motioned for her to stop. He dismounted and neared Savannah's mount, then helped her down.

"We can't take the horses any farther. There's too big a risk they'll slip. We continue on foot," he whispered.

He tied their horses before taking her hand in the darkness. "Come. We have a ways to go. If Mortimer is nearby, he has the advantage, and we'll scare him off with our talking."

She nodded, then lifted her skirts as she began to walk. "Lead the way," she whispered.

Cautiously, he moved into the dense brush. They weren't too far from the small cave, but if the pair were still there, it would be because they hadn't heard anyone approaching. Mortimer had the advantage by being above them. Gabriel had brought a lantern but didn't dark light it lest the villain see the glow.

However, even if Mortimer did see or hear them coming, he wouldn't get far. Not with a young boy in tow. Their best chance was to hope they weren't heard. Gabriel already had a plan in mind of how they would approach the area, though he hadn't thought Savannah would be so insistent in coming. She would slow him down. Hopefully, not too much.

The terrain became more and more rocky. Walking became harder. He extended a hand to Savannah to help her keep her balance. Coming upon a brook, he knew they weren't far from the cave. He pointed in the direction of the small opening and pressed a finger to his lips to assure Savannah would remain quiet.

They stood beneath an oak and listened. He wasn't quite sure for what. A noise, any indication someone was near. He motioned for Savannah to stay where she was as he carefully made his way up the rest of the path. Facing the mouth of the small cave, he stood his ground. He was met with silence. He pressed on, finding inside the remains of a fire, just recently extinguished. The embers were still warm.

They'd just missed them.

Or had they? A groan from deeper inside caught his attention. Gabriel moved farther inside, a pistol cocked and ready at his side. It was a small area carved out in the rocks. The sound of another moan drew him in. He had no light and needed a torch or something similar to see. It was the sound of a child.

Not knowing whether Dawson lurked in the shadows waiting to attack, Gabriel sucked in a breath, lit the lantern, and continued in the dimly lit cave. A moment later, he almost tripped over something. It felt like a body. As he bent down, he heard another sound. He had found him! Vincent was alive and safe. He bundled the boy in his arms and made his way back toward where the light that filtered in.

He laid him down at the cave opening. The boy was asleep, obviously drugged to keep him quiet. They needed to get him to the castle and have a doctor fetched. They would take him to Brook Fall; it was closer.

Gabriel was about to call for Savannah when he heard a scuffling out in the open. His body went into protection mode like a lion defending his pride. As his eyes adjusted to the light, he was only able to make out the figure of Mortimer Dawson bending over Savannah, pistol in hand.

"You came and ruined everything," he spat. "I lost everything thanks to your husband. He promised me riches and left me with nothing. *I* should be earl, not Roland's American brat. The title belongs to me!"

Savannah stilled, her eyes cold and uncaring. "It's rightfully Vincent's and you know it. Now let me up, or you're going to wish you had."

"What are you going to do? Women belong at home, not out in the middle of nowhere."

"I would be home if you hadn't taken my son."

He snorted. "When I'm finished with you and your son, people will thank me. A proper Englishman will be earl once more. It's a pity I'm going to have to mistake you for a wild beast." He raised his pistol.

Gabriel's steps quickened. As he came out of the dark and into the light, Savannah struggled in Mortimer's hold. Mortimer got off a shot, but it missed Savannah, who fought wildly with her free hand to find something beneath her skirts. Before Mortimer could straighten himself, another shot rang out. The man was caught off guard, disbelief twisting his features as he fell to the ground.

Gripped in Savannah's hands was the small pistol. She'd ridden out with the pistol hidden under her skirts, and it paid off. Roland Dawson lay dead on the ground beside her, a single shot to his heart.

Gabriel rushed over and took the weapon from Savannah's trembling hands before helping her to her feet. She clung to him as he led her away. "He was going to kill Vincent and me. It was never about the ransom. He wanted the earldom."

"I heard."

"I killed him, Gabriel," she said, passing a wide-eyed gaze over Mortimer's lifeless body.

"You were protecting your son and yourself."

"I was protecting you as well," she said, biting her lip. "Though I don't know if he knew you were here."

"It doesn't matter. It is over."

She clutched his arms. "Vincent! Did you find Vincent?"

"I did. He's been drugged, obviously to keep him quiet. I truly think Dawson had no real plan, and his threat was merely one made to keep him from being caught. At least in his eyes."

He led her to her son. She sank to the cold earth and took him in her arms, cradling him. Tears of relief streamed down her face.

"Come, let me carry him," Gabriel said. "My house is closer. We'll ride there, and I'll have someone bring the doctor."

She nodded and let him assist her to her feet. He gently picked Vincent up, and the pair began the walk to where their horses stood waiting for them. Vincent never stirred, and during their ride back to Brook Fall, Gabriel wondered just how much sleeping potion the boy had been given.

They rode in silence, Savannah keeping close to his gelding. "Why doesn't he wake up?"

"I believe he'll sleep off whatever Dawson gave him. He should be fine, but I'll have a doctor called to check him out."

"We were lucky, Gabriel. How did you know to look there?"

"It was somewhere we sometimes played as boys. I hadn't been in years because of the terrain, so I never thought to send anyone until earlier."

"Thank goodness you remembered."

"Let us put it behind us. Everyone is safe and Dawson will never be a threat again."

The castle came into view like some old fortress. As they rode into the inner sanctum of Brook Fall, they were met by servants and volunteers alike. Gabriel began shouting orders as he brought the horse to a halt and quickly got down.

As he gazed down at young Vincent lying in his arms, he noticed the boy's eyelids fluttering. He looked at his surroundings, then at Gabriel, then Savannah, who'd come to Gabriel's side as he walked to the door.

"You really do live in a castle," Vincent muttered as he fell back to sleep.

"He's going to be just fine," Gabriel said, smiling down at Savannah.

He led them inside and up the staircase. Finding the room he'd occupied after university before his father died, Gabriel lay the boy down on the bed. Savannah got onto the bed from the other side and held him in her arms. For the second time, Gabriel watched as tears filled her eyes.

"Please get word to Sky View that Vincent has been

found. Lady Dorset will want to know," Savannah said quietly.

"Don't worry about a thing. Focus on Vincent. The doctor has been sent for and everyone is being notified," Gabriel smoothed his hand over her hair, then put his arm around her while she cradled Vincent against her chest.

She nodded, still stroking her son's forehead. "I thank God you remembered that cave."

He kissed her gently. "I have some matters I need to attend to. Rest. The doctor will be here soon. I'll leave a footman outside the door in case you require anything."

He hurried down the stairs, barking orders as he went, making sure everything he needed done was taken care of. When he retreated to his study to write down some of the day's events, he found his hand shaking and his emotions high. They had been extremely lucky to find Vincent. The continued use of laudanum on a boy of Vincent's size could have had an entirely different outcome. He walked over to a sideboard where he kept a variety of spirits. Brandy, whiskey, sherry. He chose the decanter of whiskey and began to pour himself a glass. He faintly heard the door open behind him.

"Pour me one, and don't be cheap about it. It's been a hell of a day," Parr said as he came up beside him. "Thank God the boy has been found."

"Yes," he replied as he handed his friend a glass.

He poured one for himself and sat in front of the fireplace, then waited for his friend to say something more.

"I imagine Lady Dorset will arrive shortly," Parr said.

Gabriel nodded. "I'm sure she will."

"How is the boy?"

Taking a long drink of whiskey, Gabriel sat back in

the overstuffed leather chair. "Sleeping. Dawson drugged him. Laudanum, no doubt. He woke for a brief moment, but fell back asleep."

"He's young, he'll be fine."

"I'm sure he will be," he replied as he rose to pour another drink.

"What happened out there?"

He nodded. "Savannah killed Mortimer." He smiled. "Evidently, her late husband taught her to use a pistol and to hide one under her skirts."

"She was lucky—and smart."

"She was, because I have no doubt Dawson would have killed her given the chance."

"No need to ponder that, Gabriel. The important thing is Dawson won't bother either of them again."

"No, he won't."

"Come, let us toast Mrs. Dawson!" Parr crowed.

CHAPTER 24

Savannah woke to the glorious sound of her young son at her side trying to wake her. His voice was probably the most precious thing she could recall, one that she'd never take for granted.

"Mama, the duke lives in a castle. No one has castles in America."

She opened her eyes to his excited eyes as he sat near. "Yes, he does. Have you been exploring?"

He looked at her sheepishly. "Just a little. A footman went with me. He showed me around so I wouldn't get lost."

"That's nice, but the doctor wants you to rest today."

"But I did, Mama. I slept all night, and you did too."

She sat up. She still wore the same dress from yesterday. "So I did."

"Grandmama came. She sat in that chair for a long time," he said, pointing to a dark green chair.

"I wonder if she stayed or if she left?"

"Darren said she left late last night for Sky View."

"Who's Darren?" she asked as she stood.

"The footman."

"Ahhhh, I see. Why don't we have him take you

downstairs to the breakfast room? I'll be down in a couple of minutes."

"Okay, Mama. I'll tell His Grace to wait on you too."

She hadn't intended to fall asleep, not to mention sleeping that long. She hoped Gabriel had finally gotten a good night's sleep as well.

Vincent skipped out of the room while Savannah took care of her personal needs. She washed her face with water left in a pitcher. She finally gave up on her hair and let it flow free. After breakfast, she would return to Sky View for a bath and to change.

She entered the breakfast room finding Vincent and Gabriel in the midst of lively discussion. Vincent was listening to him give him the history of the fortress, asking questions that Gabriel gladly answered.

For having been kidnapped for several days, Vincent seemed no worse for wear. He was a strong boy, having gotten through the news of his own father's death without incident. Sometimes Savannah wondered if he wasn't bottling it all up inside him, and that one day it would all come spilling out. It was more than any child should have to be burdened with.

Gabriel rose from his chair the moment he saw her enter the breakfast room. Vincent did the same, mimicking the duke's every move.

"Good morning. I trust you slept well," he said with a lopsided grin she loved.

"I did, thank you. I didn't mean to fall asleep so early."

"You were exhausted. I didn't have the heart to wake you, even when Lady Dorset came."

"I recall her coming into the room, the doctor too, but little more."

"Your body needed to rest," he replied.

She sat down and instructed the footman what she

wanted. "And you, did you sleep well?" she asked Gabriel.

"Yes. I didn't wake until my valet came into the room. Usually, I'm up before he enters."

"Then you were exhausted as well, Your Grace."

She nodded to the footman as he set her plate down. Coddled eggs, sausage, and toast. It all looked heavenly, and she was hungry.

"I'm going to tour the castle when we're finished here. Parr still remains, though he's left with the constable. He wanted to see the spot..." He didn't finish, not wanting to bring up the matter in front of Vincent.

"I need to return to Sky View to bathe and change."

"No need. Lady Dorset brought your lady's maid and whatever it is you ladies need last night. I'll have Mrs. White show you to the duchess's suite when you're ready."

"Thank you," she replied.

"Come on, Your Grace. I'm ready, are you?" young Vincent asked. He was most impatient to have the duke's full attention.

"Yes. Why don't you meet me in the grand gallery. I'll be there in a few minutes."

Vincent nodded his head of sable-brown hair and skipped out of the room.

Gabriel waited until the door closed before he came around the table and kissed Savannah.

"What's that for?" she asked demurely.

"Because I love you."

"I love you too, Gabriel."

He stood up to his full height. He was a tall man, taller than Roland by three inches at least. He was muscular and tanned from all his outdoor activities. But what made her heartbeat speed was those emerald green eyes of his as they gazed at her full of love. "I intend to see about a special license this afternoon. I'm planning on riding to see the bishop today."

"You are? Have you decided when we'll marry too?"

"As soon as possible," he replied. "If you want to go to London for a dress, let me know. We can leave as soon as this Dawson matter is finished."

She shook her head. She didn't want to be away from Vincent—not at this time. "Not necessary. I have a dress in mind. I think you'll approve."

"I'm sure I will," he replied. He winked at her. "You're a beautiful woman with good taste."

"The sooner we marry, the better, Gabriel."

"Why's that?"

"Because every time you make love to me is a chance for me to conceive your child."

"Is there anything wrong with that?"

"Absolutely not. I look forward to having your child grow in my belly. I just hope you don't find me too un-attractive when I am huge with child."

"Never! Now if you'll excuse me, I have an anxious young man waiting," he replied. "Feel free to stay as long as you want. I want you to be comfortable here."

She nodded. "Thank you. Now go."

"One last thing. I thought perhaps we could sit down with Vincent and tell him our plans."

"I think that's an excellent idea, but let's give him a day or two before we spring changes on him."

He smiled. "As you wish. I'll see you later." He turned and headed out the door. Savannah watched his retreating figure and smiled.

~

WHY HADN'T she told him she suspected she already carried his child? Her mother had taught her that men didn't need to know these things until a woman was completely sure. At one time, she would have agreed with her, but with Gabriel, things were different than they had been with Roland.

Gabriel wasn't afraid of expressing his feelings with her. He loved her and therefore loved Vincent. He loved her unconditionally and would move heaven and earth for her. She knew that with all her heart.

Mrs. White showed her to the duchess's suite, which had obviously been cleaned and aired out quite recently. The furniture was French, a popular style at the moment. An arrangement of roses from the duke's garden graced one table. She walked to the window and looked out. The view was spectacular; the large meadow seemed to go on forever before it met up with the tree line in the distance. The wall that surrounded the castle hid the formal gardens that Gabriel's grand-mother had started. It was a pity something so beau-tiful wasn't easily shared nor seen.

"Can I get you anything else, madam?" Mrs. White asked.

"No, thank you."

"I hear Abbott in the bathing chamber. I can let her know you're ready."

She shook her hair, which flowed around her shoul-ders. "That's not necessary Mrs. White," she replied. "I wanted to thank you and the staff for everything you did during the search for my son. I'll never forget it."

"You're most welcome, and we look forward to the day you and His Grace marry."

"Yes, well, if he has anything to do with it, the cere-mony will take place very soon."

"Then I best make sure the silver is polished and everything is perfect."

Mrs. White turned to leave, and as soon as the door shut, Savannah made her way through a doorway and found the bathing chamber.

It amazed her how Gabriel had renovated the castle to include plumbing and hot and cold water. Gas lights were a work in progress and he'd recently bought a brand-new range for the kitchen.

She undressed as Norma scurried around the room laying out new under garments, then picking up those that were dirty. Savannah neared the large porcelain tub, taking in the scent of lilacs. She stepped into the tub and sank into the water until it was to her neck. She leaned against the back and closed her eyes.

"Would you like me to brush your hair before you wash it, madam?" Norma asked her from somewhere behind her. At one point, the idea of someone wanting to comb her hair, let alone be in her bathing chamber with her, would have caused her to jump. It was now a welcome sound. She wondered if Gabriel would ever visit her here.

Savannah nodded. "Please."

She sat back and relaxed after her hair was washed. The water was growing tepid, and she knew she'd better force herself out. Today would be a busy day for everyone.

It seemed she had a wedding to plan.

CHAPTER 25

A week later, the couple stood in the family chapel, which had been used for generations to celebrate marriages, births, and occasionally, the sorrow of death. Today was one of the days meant to celebrate.

The priest stood with Gabriel as they waited for the bride to come down the aisle to meet him. His friend, Parr, the earl of Wexford stood next to him.

There she was, dressed in a lavender dress, her hair swept up, flowers placed throughout. She was the most exquisite woman Gabriel had ever laid eyes on. In a few minutes, she would be his forever. They would share an incredible life together, have children, and yes, life's cycle would go on, but it was his life. His and Savannah's, and now another Armstrong would grace the world. Savannah shared the news with him last night she was with child. It was her wedding gift to him. A better gift he could not imagine existed.

Walking down the short aisle, she was escorted by the young Earl of Dorset, who, upon seeing Gabriel, broke into a huge grin. The boy and he shared a special bond since that day he carried the young man up the stairs to his old room. It pleased Gabriel no end. For now, in this moment, his soon-to-be son was taking his role as his mother's escort very seriously.

She nodded to her son once she was standing next to Gabriel. Vincent flashed another grin in Gabriel's direction before leaving to go sit with his grandmother, the Dowager Countess of Dorset. The attendees were small in number, on purpose. Two of the duke's other friends were in attendance as well. Henry Littleton, the Marquess of Dover and as well as John Long, Viscount of Norton. He only wished his sisters and brother could have attended, but his sister's voyage had been delayed, and the other he'd yet to hear from. Gregory, well, Gregory was having a grand old time on the Continent, he was sure. Thus, Gabriel knew not to expect him.

"Dearly beloved, we are gathered here today..." the priest boomed.

Gabriel glanced at his bride out of the corner of his eye. Her back ramrod straight, she looked past the priest. He sensed she was nervous and quietly took her hand to steady her nerves. She smiled for a second before returning her complete attention to the man in front of them.

Her voice rang strong and steady as did his as they both recited their vows. With the priest pronouncing them husband and wife, he turned to his bride, leaned down, and kissed her. The kiss lasted probably longer than was proper, but he didn't care. She was his, his wife and duchess.

Placing his bride's hand on his forearm, he walked with her down the aisle to the back of the chapel. He escorted Savannah to a small room in the back where documents for her to sign sat on a desk.

The party walked back to the castle for the wedding breakfast. Vincent had run ahead, proud of the fact he was being allowed to sit with the adults this morning.

After what the boy had endured, his parents only thought it fitting that he join them in the celebration.

"You look beautiful, Your Grace," he whispered.

"Thank you," came her reply.

"Good enough to ravage," he said playfully.

"We have guests, Gabriel," she teased.

"Ah yes, about our guests. Lady Dorset and Vincent will be leaving shortly for Dorset Manor, where Vincent will spend the night. The rest of my friends will be departing after the wedding breakfast as well. So you see, Your Grace, we will have the remainder of the day to ourselves."

She arched a brow and continued to walk. "Think you're pretty smart planning it all out, do you?"

"I do. I intend to carry you to my bed and ravage you the rest of the day and into the night."

"Gabriel, stop. This isn't the sort of conversation to be having among family and friends. Someone might overhear," she teased."

He patted her hand. "Trust me, my dear, everyone knows where we'll be the remainder of the day."

"Yes, I'm sure they do," she said biting her lip to stop from smiling.

They walked in silence for a few minutes. He purposely slowed, allowing everyone to pass them. No one thought a thing about it, and in a matter of minutes, not one person other than themselves were on the path.

He leaned down to kiss her. She opened to him, and his tongue urged hers to merge. He pressed himself against her, knowing if it weren't for the fact they were expected, he would take her right now. He would take her somewhere hidden, of course, but he would have her.

"We should go," she whispered.

"You're right," he replied. "How are you feeling?"

"I feel better than I have in ages, and it's all thanks to you."

He kissed her again. "I love you, Savannah. You are my strength and my weakness. I look forward to spending the rest of my life with you."

"I love you too." And she did. With all her heart. Never had she felt such deep, devoted feelings for one man—her husband.

They began to walk again, their first as man and wife. This coming year would be filled with firsts, including the birth of his first child. How much better could life get for a duke and his American wife?

EPILOGUE

Gabriel Robert Charles Armstrong entered the world red-faced and screaming. Just born, already the babe seemed to know his place in the world and demanded those around him meet his needs.

Savannah stared down at her son as the midwife placed him in her arms. She'd wanted to name him after her father and Roland, but as Gabriel explained, his first-born son would carry his name. She gracefully gave in once he agreed the child would be known as Robert.

"How do you feel?" he asked her as he peered down at his son.

"Tired."

"I imagine that's to be expected. If you'd like, the nurse can take him."

"No, I would rather have some time with you and Robert."

He smiled. "I imagine Vincent's going to scold us both for not sending for him."

"Which is why I sent him to stay with his grandmother. We'll send word first thing in the morning."

"Yes, we will."

"Would you like to hold him?" she asked as she watched him closely.

"May I?"

"Of course! He's your son. My hope is that you'll spend lots of time with him."

He shifted nervously and bent down to take the babe she offered. Gabriel peered down at his firstborn. He certainly did resemble an Armstrong with the same goldish-brown hair. He walked around the bedchamber, his son in his arms.

The babe stared up at Gabriel as though he already knew who he was. A duke and his heir, the cycle of life repeating itself.

PREVIEW ONCE UPON A COUNTESS

CHAPTER 1

The carriage, pulled by four perfectly matched white horses, drew up outside the towering classical facade of Clevedon House, the London residence of the Duke of Clevedon. If it weren't for the fact that the duke was a close friend from their days at Eaton and Cambridge, Parr would have declined the invitation. The night, however, was important to Clevedon. It was the first dinner party held by the recently married duke and duchess, and Parr could never refuse Clevedon. The duke had assured him the affair would be small, knowing Parr disliked large, crowded events.

His own sister, Alexandria, reminded him he needed to host some sort of social event as well. As the Earl of Wexford, Parr needed to expand his social horizons beyond White's and mistresses. Alexandria was of the opinion that he needed a wife and promised him she would put together a tasteful affair. He escaped a lengthy discussion over who he should invite for the time being. That had proved easy enough. He'd merely promised her he would give the matter serious consideration.

Clevedon and his charming wife, Savannah, Her

Grace The Duchess of Clevedon, were waiting inside the door, in the grand hall. His friend the duke had fallen head over heels in love with the charming American and her young son. A tale to be savored another time. He needed to focus his attention on his hosts.

"Clevedon," he murmured before turning his attention to the duchess. He bowed slightly. "You look as beautiful as ever, Your Grace."

"Thank you, Dear Wexford, and thank you for accepting our invitation. My husband says you're not fond of large social events."

He smiled. "He would be correct. I find I dislike the crush of the endless balls and soirees."

"May I tell you a secret?" she asked with her prominent American accent. "I'm not fond of them either, so your secret is safe with me."

Clevedon cut in. "I believe you'll be fine, Parr. There are several guests you know, and my wife managed to keep the affair small."

Parr nodded and again gave the duchess a slight bow before he walked off in the direction of the drawing room. Champagne was being served, and he took a flute from the tray of a passing footman. Taking a long sip, he walked through the doors.

He found there were, by his count, ten couples in total, plus one young woman who appeared to be on her own, without an escort. Perhaps one of the duchess's friends or some distant relation of the duke's. In either case, he was intrigued. The young woman obviously had a season or two behind her. She was comfortable conversing with those around her.

She was an exquisite creature. Her ginger hair was swept up off her neck. A long, luxurious neck, one that was made for kissing. She wore a deep-sapphire-colored silk gown. Pearls adorned that beautiful neck. She looked like a queen or, in his case, a countess. That was absurd. He wasn't looking for a wife, even though everyone told him it was past time.

Clevedon came to his side, observing the festivities. "I see you've found Lady Clare."

"Lady Clare?"

"Yes, the beauty in the dark blue gown."

Parr finished his champagne and took another from one of many footmen. "Who accompanied her?"

"No one. She's my cousin on my mother's side. She was raised in Scotland and France."

"Really? That's fascinating. So she's not betrothed?"

"No, which is why my aunt sent her to London."

Parr arched a brow and smiled. "Tell me about her, and yes, you must introduce us."

"Don't worry, I will. I believe my wife has seated the two of you together for dinner."

"Excellent. I knew there was a reason I liked the duchess."

"Come I want to acquaint you to a few gentlemen I don't believe you know, and I'll make sure you are introduced to Lady Clare before we go into dinner."

"Excellent. What can you tell me about her before we're introduced? You said she was your cousin."

Clevedon finished the remainder of his champagne and placed the flute on a nearby table. "As I said, she's my cousin and was raised in Scotland and France. Her father, my uncle, is the Duke of Renfrew. Clare is proficient in French, Gaelic and Italian, she can ride better than most men I know, she paints and is far more proficient on pianoforte."

Parr nodded as he listened. "What of her temperament?"

His friend smiled ever so slightly. "She is a delight to be around so long as you don't rile her. She's known for her fierce Scottish temper and a tart tongue."

"Lady Claire sounds quite interesting. I look forward to getting to know her better."

"Come, let me introduce you before we get weighted down in some political discussion."

They walked across the drawing room to where Lady Clare was surrounded by Viscount Newton's wife, Lady Newton and Countess Taylor. Her husband, the Earl of Taylor was well known as a successful land baron with property throughout England and Wales.

"Ladies, I would like to present Parr, the Earl of Wexford," Clevedon said. "Wexford, I believe you already know Countess Taylor and Lady Newton."

"I do. Ladies, nice seeing you this evening."

"Wexford, may I present my cousin, Lady Clare."

Parr nodded, took the hand Lady Clare offered. "Lady Clare, I'm pleased to meet you."

She studied him for a moment, her pale blue eyes sizing him up. "I'm sure you are, Lord Wexford. Everyone is."

Wexford arched a brow. "I beg pardon, my lady?"

She did something with her eyes. Did she actually roll her eyes at him? Clevedon hadn't mentioned her being a snob.

Lady Clare opened her fan, then closed it. "My father, the Duke of Renfrew is quite wealthy, and unfortunately I find most men use me as a way to get in my father's good graces."

"I can assure you I live quite comfortably, and what your father has or may not have is not my concern."

"Then you are a first, Lord Wexford. A man with no interest in my father. How refreshing."

"If you ladies will excuse us," Clevedon said. "Lord Hemsley is beckoning us."

Wexford bowed. "Ladies a pleasure as always. Lady Clare, it has been good to meet one of Clevedon's Scottish relations."

The two men turned and left the ladies. They strode across the large room toward a small group of gentlemen, Lord Hemsley among them.

"So that's your cousin."

The edge of Clevedon's mouth curved up. "I warned you. She thinks any man who shows interest in her is simply wanting to get closer to the duke."

"Her tongue is enough to scare off most men."

"Indeed. She's had two proposals. Both she refused, and her father didn't approve of one. He allowed her the other refusal. Like I said her father wishes her wed."

Parr snorted. "I do believe I've heard of your cousin. Her dowry's reportedly the largest in all England and Scotland."

"Her name and dowry precede her. I'm afraid it's worn on my cousin."

"I can see where it might."

They neared the group of men, stopping just short of joining them. "You'll get to know her better at dinner. Just don't bring up money and you should be safe from her wrath."

"I'll try to remember that." Parr glanced across the room and saw the duchess had joined the group. Unfortunately, Lady Clare's back was to him, and he couldn't see her face. Dinner would be shortly and he would have his chance to get to know the lady better then.

ALSO BY JR SALISBURY

MAYFAIR

Dealing with the Duchess

Ravaging the Duke

To Love An Earl

The Marquess Takes A Bride

MACLEODS OF SKYE

Donnan's Rose

The Sins of Rory MacLeod

Lord Malcolm's Heart

Taming Lily

The Wicked Seduction of Wallace MacLeod

LOVE AND DEVOTION

Wish Upon A Duke

Once Upon A Countess

Seduction of a Duke

Second Chance At Love

ABOUT THE AUTHOR

J. R. Salisbury is the historical romance alter-ego of contemporary romance author Jamie Salisbury. Writing romance stories with passion and sass, Jamie Salisbury has seen several of her books soar to #1 on Amazon. Her novella, Tudor Rubato was a finalist in the 2012 RONE awards. The cover won for Best Contemporary Cover. In 2014, her novel, Life and Lies was nominated for a RONE in the Erotica category. Her books are self published.

Music, traveling and history are among her passions when not writing. Her previous career in public relations in and around the entertainment field has afforded her with a treasure trove of endless story ideas.

Follow Jamie:
Book + Main
Website

Facebook as Jamie Salisbury